DETROIT PUBLIC LIBRARY

3 5674 0

W9-DDN-476

"A   odel
of   Mr.
Est   nost
pra   ples
of   view

"A   ould
und   n my
ver   d for
ple

"Fo   more
Le   He's
tha

"T   s use
of   like
Isa

Fawcett Crest Books
by Loren D. Estleman:

ANGEL EYES

KILL ZONE

MOTOR CITY BLUE

ANGEL EYES

Loren D. Estleman

FAWCETT CREST • NEW YORK

P.B

Library of Congress Catalog Card Number: 81-4664

ISBN 0-449-21134-7

First published by Houghton Mifflin Company
Reprinted by permission of Houghton Mifflin Company

Manufactured in the United States of America

First Ballantine Books Edition: January 1987

KN

FEB   '87

To my mother and father,
for all the right reasons

1

THE CRESCENT WAS A CELLAR PLACE ON CASS, ESTABlished before Michigan outlawed public dining and drinking below ground level. A door with an iron grille left over from Prohibition led down a short flight of steps into a bin full of noise and smoke, in the center of which a half-naked pubescent blonde was shaking her various appendages to the disco beat while lights changed her exposed flesh from green to orange to blue and back to green. The music sounded like an old lady shaking her teeth in a glass.

In the absence of a hostess I groped my way along the buzzing concrete floor until I found an empty table and ordered a double Scotch. Ringside, the light show cast ghastly hues over glistening male faces wreathed in marijuana smoke, their watery eyes following the dancer's bumps and grinds, white-tipped tongues sliding along fat, grinning lips. On the outer fringe, almost in darkness, a couple of guys were kissing at a table.

The gyrating blonde's was one of only two white faces in the room; the other belonged to me. But hers wasn't the face I'd been told to look for, so when the waiter returned I asked him if he'd seen Ann Maringer.

"Lots of times," came the sullen reply. "She works here."

I looked up at him. He was a big black with lumpy shoulders under his red uniform shirt and a shot of gray in his gnarled black hair. His eyes, bright white semicircles beneath an apish brow, had the slightly knocked-out-of-focus look you sometimes see in boxers who stayed too long in the ring. I said, "Have you seen her tonight?"

"Who wants to know?"

"Me and the Wayne County Sheriff's Department." I flashed the buzzer the department had forgotten about, carefully lest the sight of it empty the room; it was that kind of place. He squinted at it a moment, then jerked a broad flat thumb over his shoulder. As he did so, the light show died, to be replaced by a single baby spot that washed the empty platform in powdery blue. The tiny electrified combo hurled itself into the first three beats of a fresh piece. A new dancer took up the position.

"Just don't bust her in front of the clientele," the waiter advised. "The boss don't like scenes."

"No busts. Just talk."

He nodded solemnly and moved off into the gloom with the ponderous grace of an aging elephant.

She was a blonde, like her predecessor, but that was where the similarity ended. She was thin, almost bony, and her hair, unlike the other's stringy, waist-length locks, was done up frothily on either side of her head like water boiling around the base of a fall. The style had been popular about the time the first dancer was born, which tied in with this one's apparent age. She wasn't too old to be wearing her brief costume of spangled fringe with a bare midriff, but the dance she was doing fit her the way a screw top fits a bottle of champagne. Still, she gave it something it hadn't had originally, moving with a controlled fever that suggested a lifetime spent undulating to sour, secondhand arrangements played by sullen, third-rate bands. The overhead spot painted hollows beneath her eyes and in her cheeks, accentuating her gauntness.

I concentrated on the music. Somewhere under all that crap, a strain or two from the old Sinatra hit "Angel Eyes" struggled toward the surface from time to time, only to be put under again by the pounding drums and snarling electric guitars. But she knew it was there, and that was all that counted.

The music ended abruptly and she was left in darkness

to find her own way down to the floor. There was no applause. I was wondering if I was supposed to meet her in the dressing room and where that might be when she appeared at my table, still in costume.

"Amos Walker?" Her voice was low-register, not quite husky. When I stood: "You're better-looking than I'd hoped. I was expecting Mike Hammer."

"Disappointed?"

She smiled briefly, without committing herself. Away from the stage, her face was hard, its natural angularity heightened by sharp creases beneath her eyes and at the corners of her thin mouth. But the eyes themselves were large and blue and childlike, untouched by time and experience. Against the life-map of her face they looked like fresh replacements. The tune she danced to had been no random choice.

Her baby blues swept the immediate vicinity, taking in the black faces that were turned in our direction. "Let's find a booth. This is worse than being on stage."

We wedged ourselves into a coffinlike cubicle near the door, upholstered in slippery vinyl and illuminated not at all by a tiny electric lamp posing as a candle on the burn-scarred table. The bruiser who had waited on me earlier lumbered forward out of the shadows. She ordered vodka neat. I asked for a refill and a flashlight. He left with an expression that told me he'd heard that one before.

"Nathan Washington gave me your card," Ann Maringer said. "He says you stick like nuclear fallout."

"He ought to know. I'm still dunning him for what he owes me on that tail job I did for him last year."

"That's his problem. Or yours." She took a cigarette from my proffered pack and let me light it. The glow of the flame was kind to her, softening her bony features and doing wonderful things with her eyes. A man could fall in love with eyes like those. As I lit one for myself I wondered how many had.

She watched me through the smoke. "You work late Sundays. I didn't expect anyone to answer when I called your office at ten."

3

I said nothing, particularly about falling asleep over a game of solitaire. She took my silence for professional ethics.

"You were a cop?"

I nodded. "In the service. The instructors in the Detroit Police training program didn't like me, so I went to Vietnam to forget."

"I'll bet. You drowned your sorrows killing the same people we're making instant citizens out of now."

I let that one drift. I was watching her replacement on stage, a gangling black girl with the vertebrae of a snake, cavorting to something that didn't sound much like "Up a Lazy River" anymore.

"So how come you're a private eye?"

My eyes were still ringside. "How come you're a dancer?"

She laughed shortly. "Because I find my home life a lot more comfortable with the electricity on. I'm conducting an interview here. The least you could do is pay attention to my questions."

"What do you want to know?" I asked irritably, looking at her. "I'm bonded. My fee is two hundred fifty a day plus expenses. Sometimes grief is all my clients buy. I don't guarantee even that, but I do promise a day's work for a day's pay, which means I don't belong to a union." She flinched at that. I didn't find out why until later. "Nate Washington told you I'm reliable or I wouldn't be here," I continued. "If you're shopping, my office hours are in the Yellow Pages." I started to rise. She put out a hand to stop me. There was a diamond ring on the engagement finger that would choke a goat.

The waiter brought our drinks and withdrew, ignoring the silence that was the fanfare of his occupation. When he had passed beyond earshot:

"My, you're hot-headed," she said. "You're just like— never mind. I didn't mean to sound like I was grilling you." She watched with approval as I took my first sip, advertising my intention to remain. "What are the odds of finding someone who's missing? Intact."

4

"That depends on how long he's been gone and whether he wants to be found. Generally, I prefer it when they don't."

"Why?"

"Deliberately vanishing means giving up your identity. Most people aren't prepared to go that far. They've got hobbies, interests, needs they can't abandon. With today's technology a competent investigator should be able to pick up a trail within a few days in most cases. Unless the FBI or the CIA or some other federal agency is involved in the disappearance, in which case he ought to have something in an hour or two. The more tightly the cloak-and-dagger boys try to pull wraps over something, the easier it is to uncover. It didn't used to be that way, but we only get one J. Edgar Hoover to a century."

"And if they want to be found?"

"Then we're talking kidnap, which is a different story. Abductors don't place much store in their victims' needs or interests, and unless they leave behind a button or a broken shoelace or a ransom demand I've got nothing to go on. Besides, that's a police matter, and they have strange ways of showing their appreciation for my help. Of course, all this is academic if the missing party's been gone longer than a few months. I once found a girl who hadn't been seen in nearly a year, but that was a fluke and my client wasn't at all happy with what I brought back."

She nodded, but understanding fell short of her eyes. Looking at the rest of her, it was hard to believe they were the ones she'd started out with. While listening she had held her cigarette upright between long-nailed fingers, blowing across the glowing end. The ash was an inch long before she tapped it into a cheap tin tray. Then she started in all over again.

I said, "You haven't touched your drink."

"It's only club soda." She touched her lips to the glass and set it back down with a grimace. "Part of my job is to mix with the customers and get them to buy me drinks."

"It's that kind of place, is it?"

"I've never worked in any of the other kind."

5

"Would you rather?"

She shrugged one shoulder. "My feet wouldn't hurt any less than they do here." Her eyes leaped from the cigarette to me. "Look, if it bothers you I'll pay for the drinks."

"I never let a woman pay the tab. I'll put it on my expense sheet."

She laughed again, a low, throaty sound that stirred something in me I hadn't realized was still there. Suddenly she flipped a switch and broke the circuit.

"If you could start looking for the missing party before it came up missing, what would be your chance then?"

I hesitated. "Better, I would think, without speaking from experience. They don't usually make appointments."

"Until now."

I smoked and watched her. The amplified music thundered along the floor, vibrating our glasses on the table. She took hold of hers for the first time and drank deeply. She grimaced, as if she wished it weren't just club soda.

"I'm about to disappear, Mr. Walker," she said. "Very suddenly and very soon."

"Voluntarily?"

"No."

"Have you been to the police?"

She laughed again. This time there was an edge to it. "I've danced professionally since I was fifteen. I know what cops think of dancers, and they aren't likely to spend many tax dollars looking for one that's missing. Or one that's about to be. It's one of the hazards of the profession, like rape for prostitutes. Besides, I'm a rugged individualist. I prefer to choose my own rescuer."

"You lie lousy, Miss Maringer."

Anger flushed her cheeks, only to fade when she saw it wasn't reflected in my face.

"Does it bother you?" she asked.

"I'm used to it. Only priests hear the truth first time through. I don't have their clout. When you're ready to part with it, I'm in the book."

We locked glances for a moment, like two strange cats sizing each other up in the gloom of a back alley. The nymphet who had been dancing when I came in finished a second number. The music paused for a beat, then started up again. "Angel Eyes." It made my companion anxious.

"That's my number. I'm covering for another girl. Here's my address; it's right down the street." She fished a folded scrap of paper out of the valley between her breasts and handed it to me as she got up. "I'm off at two. We'll talk there. That is, if you're interested." The blue eyes brimmed over with entreaty.

I rose. "Can you afford me, Miss Maringer?"

She glanced impatiently toward the stage and the vamping band, then, impulsively, tugged the sparkler off her finger and pressed it into my palm. "That will bring seven hundred and fifty from any honest jeweler. It's worth far more. It should buy me three days."

"After that, what?"

"After that, don't bother." She hurried away.

I turned back toward the table and almost bumped into the hulking waiter.

"Did you get an earful?" I asked him.

He handed me the bill and moved off without a word.

I finished my drink, paid, and left while she was still dancing. Pausing before the door to adjust my hat and coat, I heard someone shifting his weight on the other side and moved to make room for the customer's entrance. The door remained closed. Nerves tingling, I transferred my Smith & Wesson from its snap holster to the right-hand pocket of my coat and depressed the thumb latch on the door. It swung inward of its own weight. Someone's vaporized breath swirled in the cold air outside.

"It does my heart good to see a waiter waiting," I said.

He'd been standing on the sidewalk. Silently, with that economy of movement an athlete never forgets, he leaped down into the shallow stairwell that led up to the street. He had drawn a sheep-lined jacket on over his red shirt. And he was carrying a baseball bat.

"Gimme that ring." He brandished the club.

I fingered the gun in my pocket but decided against using it. His choice of weapons was too tempting. Taking my

7

hesitation for obstinance, he whooped and swung the bat at my head. I ducked and jabbed the stiffened fingers of my right hand into his solar plexus. His heavy jacket prevented the blow from penetrating too deeply, but he doubled over retching and I got my hands on the bat. Grasping it by both ends, I twisted it from his grip, stepped sideways, and brought my arms down over his head, pulling back and forcing the weapon against his throat.

I didn't have to do anything more, just increase the pressure and it would have been all over except the inquest. Instead, I let go of the bat and brought my right hand chopping against the side of his neck. He whimpered and oozed into a puddle at my feet.

"Never stick-fight with an ex-MP," I told the twitching mess on the landing. It was lost on him.

No one inside had heard the scuffle. I was still standing there when a flamboyantly dressed black with a white woman on his arm started coming down the stairs. He saw me and stopped. I read the emotions on his ginger face and knew that I was never going to explain the situation to his satisfaction. I sighed and aired the revolver.

The woman gasped. She was a redhead with a complexion that looked impossibly pale beside her companion's. I said, "Go in and have a good time, folks. The lounge is closed."

He considered the situation. He hadn't acquired the wherewithal to buy those clothes by taking foolish chances. I was relieved, but not surprised, when at length he tightened his grip on the woman's arm and ushered her past me without looking back. I closed the door behind him and, stepping over the waiter, sprinted for my car before a posse could be rounded up. I didn't know then how much grief that little scene would cost me.

2

IT HAD BEEN A LONG TIME SINCE MY LAST BAR FIGHT, AND by the time I got to my office on Grand River I had the shakes pretty good. I hoisted the bottle out of the desk, poured my first unwatered-down drink of the evening, and nursed it thoughtfully. Then I switched on the desk lamp and got out Ann Maringer's ring to study it. That bought me exactly nothing. Glass or not, it went into my ancient safe to await appraisal while I made another donation to my alcohol system.

I checked my watch. It was too late to go home and too early to meet my client, and in any case I didn't want to show my face there again until I was sure the lynch mob had dispersed. I propped my feet up on the desk and went to sleep.

When I awoke it was almost two o'clock. The drinks had caught up with me. My eyes ached and my mouth was glued shut. Donning Polaroids against the glare of street lights and headlights, I cranked up my battered Cutlass and took my time negotiating the labyrinth of thaw-slick streets that are Detroit in early spring. As a result I was half an hour late by the time I reached the address on Cass.

Cass Corridor. Fire Alley, the boys on the Detroit Fire Department call it, that neighborhood being the arson capital of the so-called inner city. Most people avoid it even in broad daylight, some from righteous indignation over its thriving hooker trade, others because the Cass Corridor Strangler remains at large five years after the killing ceased.

After two in the morning, when the bars and bowling alleys vomit their clientele out onto the street, the area boils briefly, then settles back into sullen dark complacency as it waits to swallow the occasional lone transient. The magic word *Renaissance* opens no doors on Cass.

Ann Maringer's building was a grimy brickfront as old as the eight-hour workday, its upper floors scorched and their windows boarded up after a recent fire, not its first. The foyer, dark but for a streak of greasy moonlight sliding through a broken pane, was strewn with cracked and curled linoleum tiles and stank of cooked cabbage. The smell grew stronger as I climbed the narrow, complaining staircase. Rats' claws clattered behind the walls as I advanced, their owners scrabbling ahead of me like nasty leaves before a fresh gust.

The apartment was on the third floor, at the end of a flyblown hall painted mustard-yellow above the wainscoting. Harsh light spilled through the open doorway over the gnawed rubber runner. Something else had spilled out with it. A man's arm.

The rest of him lay on his stomach just inside the threshold, where he had collapsed after using his last ounce of strength to reach up and pull open the door. Part of his red uniform shirt showed garishly above his sheepskin collar. I reached down and felt his neck for a pulse. I could have saved myself the trouble. He had swung his last baseball bat. His flesh was still warm. There was pink froth on his lips and his eyes were white gashes in the mottled face.

Fighting back nausea, I stepped over him into the apartment. The room was cheaply furnished but clean, except for a dark crimson smear some six inches wide matting the carpet from the body to a door on the opposite side of the room, which yawned open. This led into a bedroom just large enough to contain the object for which it was named, a stand supporting a lamp with a white china base, and a peeling dresser. Here the stink of cordite was stronger than that of the cabbage.

The top of the dresser was littered with bottles and jars containing the things women use to ward off time, nothing very costly or difficult to obtain. Woman's clothing, neatly folded, filled the drawers, their labels bearing the names of chain stores in the area. An open box of sanitary napkins lay demurely beneath a stack of nylon slips.

The unmade bed yielded nothing more interesting. There was room for only one on the narrow mattress, which would disappoint a lascivious cophouse reporter I knew on the *Free Press*. A faded pair of woman's jeans and a brown cotton pullover had been flung carelessly across the footboard. A brassiere lay on the floor beneath. Near that was a worn track shoe, too small for most men. I found its mate under the bed.

A light spring jacket hung in the narrow closet next to an empty hanger. Two pairs of shoes designed for fancier and more feminine dress than that required by the track shoes were lined up on the floor like patient sentinels. On the top shelf reposed an expensive calfskin suitcase, not new. I hoisted it down, getting dust on my clothes, and opened it. It was empty.

In the other room, besides the dead man, were the usual furniture, a carton of Bel Airs with three packs gone, magazines, dime-a-dozen landscapes in frames bolted to the walls. A black vinyl shoulder bag slouched wearily on a table near the door. Among the normal junk inside I found one of the missing cigarette packs and a wallet containing three twenties, a couple of fives, and a single. And a bank book showing a balance of three hundred and forty-six dollars.

There was no kitchen in the apartment. The bathroom would be down the hall. Something was missing. No doubt Miss Marple would finger it right away, the presence of a corpse notwithstanding. I was still working on it when I turned and spotted the uniformed cop watching me from the doorway. His youthful face looked frightened, but his gun was drawn, and in that moment I realized with an empty feeling that so was mine.

"IT'S A STINKING SHAME THEY TOOK OUR CATTLE prods."

11

The speaker was a plainclothes sergeant, black, in shirt sleeves, with a round slick face the unhealthy gray of cooked liver. The room, claustrophobic and bare but for the chair I was sitting in, was one of the interrogation cells I'd seen a dozen times at police headquarters. This was my first time in the seat of honor. I asked him what time it was. They'd taken my watch.

"Where you're going they measure time with calendars." He thrust his face to within two inches of mine. His breath smelled like an ashtray. "Like I was saying, a jab or two with one of those little electric mothers and you'd remember everything right down to the Preamble to the Constitution."

I said, "I'm surprised you've heard of it."

"Don't smart-mouth me, nigger-killer. Who's to say you didn't attack me and force me to defend myself by turning that pretty face into Silly Putty?"

I grinned. He backhanded me across the mouth. I grinned again, feeling blood trickle down my chin from my split lip. He reached back for a swipe in the other direction. His partner caught his arm.

"That's how guys get rich in this town," the partner told him calmly. "Suing the police for brutality."

Shorter than his partner but built more solidly, this one had a mop of curly yellow hair and stiff eyebrows to match, which stood out against his ruddy complexion like bristles caught in fresh paint. His light blue eyes were inclined to sparkle and his mouth was fixed in a constant tight-lipped smile. He looked like somebody's uncle.

His partner didn't think of him that way. Their gazes locked for a moment, and the gray went out of his face as suddenly as if a tap had been thrown open somewhere in his system. He said, "Okay" quietly, and his arm was released. Pouting, he rubbed circulation back into his wrist while the other handed me a handkerchief to stop the bleeding.

"You fell, right?"

I looked at him, at his twinkling eyes, and said, "Yeah, right." I mopped my chin with the handkerchief. There

12

wasn't as much blood as I'd thought. Not as much as there could have been. He watched me.

"You'll have to excuse Sergeant Cranmer. He hasn't been the same since the Miranda decision. You might say it broke his spirit." He fished a crushed pack of cigarettes out of his shirt pocket and offered me one.

"What kind?" I asked.

"Luckies."

"Forget it."

He shrugged and put away the package without taking one for himself. "It's almost five," he said, answering the question I'd forgotten about. "You've been in here an hour and a half. Too long to stick with that story you gave us." His voice was soothing.

"But long enough to run a ballistics test on the slug you dug out of the waiter's body and prove it didn't come from my gun," I replied. "And your good cop, bad cop routine has whiskers."

His smile faltered, and for a moment it looked as if he might cuff me himself. But his gyroscope held true. Calmly he said, "We're still waiting for the report, but it's a fact your gun hadn't been fired recently. It wouldn't be the first time a job was done with a throwaway piece, ditched in favor of another weapon for protection."

"Brilliant deduction, Lieutenant. I bet in high school you used a corkscrew for a slide rule."

"You were seen fighting with the victim earlier, after which you made your escape in a blue '70 Cutlass, license number GJZ-600. The uniform who took that report spotted the vehicle parked in front of the apartment building and found you standing over the victim with a gun in your hand. The apartment's being searched and I've got men combing the alley next to the building. When they find a murder weapon we'll see what we can do about bringing back capital punishment in this state."

I didn't like it. His case was flimsy as a hotel room chair, but if the killer had happened to dump the widow-maker in the vicinity, I wouldn't see daylight for a week. "Who called the cops?"

13

His smile was blandly diabolical. "Nice try, Walker. This department doesn't invest in revenge."

"What's my motive? I won the fight."

"Maybe that wasn't enough. Maybe you were interrupted before you had a chance to finish the job and came back later to follow him until a better opportunity arose."

"Maybe you're bucking for captain and don't want too many unsolved murders mucking up your record. Or maybe you know who did it and you're working on a bonus."

"Maybe you fell down again and swallowed your teeth," spat Sergeant Cranmer, charging. His partner flung out an arm to stop him. I smiled and shook my head.

"You cops remind me of a cocker I had when I was a kid. He only knew one trick but he made the most of it. I'm sorry as hell, but I'm fresh out of treats."

The lieutenant swore for the first time since he'd entered the room. "You're all alike, you private guys. So busy grubbing up a buck you start forgetting who your friends are. We can give you protection if you'll open up. What do you think Phil Montana's going to do when he finds out?"

I looked at him blankly. "Where does Montana figure in? Was the waiter a steelhauler?"

"Not hardly. He wasn't a waiter either, not full time. His name was Bendigo Adams Jefferson, a.k.a. Bingo the Bat, after his favorite method of persuasion. He had the makings of a champion heavyweight back in the sixties until they caught him selling dope and sent him up for ten years. In Jackson he got in tight with Montana when Phil was up on that assault rap, and after his release Montana made him his personal bodyguard. Having Bingo with him had a lot to do with his getting back on top of United Steelhaulers. If you didn't know all that before you croaked Jefferson, his pockets were full of identification. Your dumb show is older than our good cop, bad cop."

"I didn't have a chance to go over the stiff." I considered. "A guy in his position must have had a lot of enemies. My killing him over a theft attempt makes a pretty big coincidence."

"Especially with a strike threatening and a lot of angry people on both sides. Which is one of the reasons I don't believe that part about his trying to mug you. Come on, Walker. He must have been pulling down thirty grand a year just for looking scary."

"It must not have been enough or he wouldn't have been moonlighting as a waiter."

"All right," he said patiently, "suppose he had expensive habits. Why jump you? You had eleven dollars in your wallet when we booked you, and this suit you're wearing went out with poems that rhyme. Old ladies gave me better excuses when I stopped them for speeding back on traffic control."

"Bet they're still doing time." I hadn't told him about the diamond ring. "Why did I pick a fight with him then? I forget."

"It's a short step from accepting money to poke around in other people's lives to accepting money to end them. Every snitch in Detroit knows there's been a contract out on Montana since he chucked the Mafia's puppet out of the top union spot. But he never goes anywhere without Bingo, so you were hired to take him out first. Either that, or it was a warning to Montana from the steel mills to toe the line. Which one is it, Walker? You tell me."

"What about Ann Maringer? Found her yet?"

"Not yet, but we will. She might be an eyewitness."

"She might," I agreed. "Which is one good reason for the killer to have taken her with him. Or with her. These are liberated times."

"It's also a good reason for her to have ducked out before you drilled her, too."

"Without her purse? That's the first thing women grab when they're in a hurry."

"Who knows what goes through a woman's mind when she's in terror for her life?" But he didn't sound convinced of that. He was too experienced not to have thought of it, but my mentioning it bothered him even more.

"How come no one in the building reported hearing a shot?" He clucked his tongue. He was on solid ground

15

again. "In that neighborhood? Besides, this is a big department; we've heard of silencers. I even got to touch one once."

"Here's something else to chew on," I said. "Why weren't there any personal articles in the entire apartment? No pictures, nothing. I frisked her purse. No ID. Not even so much as an expired driver's license or a reminder of a dental appointment. Didn't that make you the least bit curious?"

"Curiosity," he mused. "I think I left that next to my virginity. We're checking out that angle. Maybe she's not who she says she is. From where I'm standing that doesn't make you look any more innocent."

The sparring was starting to wear on me. I was beginning to feel guilty, worrying that I'd let down my guard and allow him to smash my alibi to pieces. That's how cops work, like priests in reverse but with the same goal in mind: Confession. I said, "I seem to remember something about getting one telephone call."

"Jeez, I think they're all out of order," said Cranmer.

"Shut up," said the lieutenant.

The buzz of activity outside the soundproof interrogation room hurt my ears. Voices droned in the squad room, paper whispered, telephone bells jangled, a hunt-and-pecker plucked desultorily at the keys of an ancient Underwood typewriter. Under the watchful eye of a fresh-looking cop in uniform I bonged two borrowed dimes into a pay telephone and punched out Lieutenant John Alderdyce's home number. He was better than a lawyer any day.

16

3

THE NEXT ROUND OF QUESTIONS WAS INTERRUPTED BY A knock at the interrogation room door. Cranmer poked his head inside and whispered in the lieutenant's ear. "Shit!" exclaimed his superior, pushing past him. The door was pulled shut. Alone in the room, I fell asleep on the hard chair and dreamed of men with holes in their chests dragging themselves through gory slicks, pink bubbles forming inside their nostrils and at the corners of their mouths. I awoke with my hands gripping the legs of my chair to find John Alderdyce glowering at me from the doorway. I rubbed my eyes with my thumbs and ran my fingers through my hair to clear out the snarls. I wondered how much more gray there was in it this morning.

"Thanks for coming down, John. I owe you."

"Forget it," he said. "Forget me. Please. There's nothing I like better than coming back to the station ten hours before I have to. Do me a favor and forget I ever lived."

A coarse-featured black man with as much eye for fashion as one can entertain on a detective lieutenant's salary, John had settled in his haste for a shirt that looked as if he'd worn it all through the four P.M. to midnight shift, under a tailored brown safari jacket five shades lighter than his trousers. But his necktie appeared fresh. We'd met twenty years before, when his father and mine went into partnership in a west side garage. Not that we could be called friends in our respective professions.

I said, "Did you get my bail ticket?"

17

"I got your freedom, not that I've got anything against Renaissance. Fitzroy's letting you go."

"Fitzroy?"

"You just spent two hours with him. Weren't you introduced?"

"We may have been. I'm punchy. Did you leave any marks?"

"No rough stuff. Just logic." He was still boiling. "They can't find a murder weapon and the woman who reported your fight with Bingo Jefferson refuses to sign a statement."

"A woman," I reflected. "Redhead, nice build, medium height?"

"You saw her, then."

"With her pimp. Anything else?"

"They haven't found the killer, if that's what you mean."

"I was thinking of Ann Maringer."

"We could be talking about the same person."

"I thought about that. I don't think so."

He put that one on a back burner. "What did you say to Fitzroy? He doesn't usually turn that shade of purple just because a case goes sour."

I shrugged. "I got a little smart. Sue me. He was only trying to ram Murder One down my throat."

A cop in uniform came up behind Alderdyce. "Excuse me, Lieutenant, but we need the room for a rapist."

"Put it to music and go to Nashville." He looked back at me. "My office."

We detoured downstairs to reclaim my stuff from the front desk. The sergeant there, a bifocaled veteran with four stars on his sleeve and crew-cut hair the color of rusted steel, told me they were holding onto my gun for the time being. I said I'd ask his captain about that. He replied that I could do something vile with a duck for all he cared. On our way back up we met Lieutenant Fitzroy coming down, in corduroy topcoat and a narrow-brimmed hat that made him look like an economy-size leprechaun.

"Try to get past the city limits," he told me. "Just try.

18

You'll be ass-deep in law before your foot touches ground."

John said, "Stop playing dick, Fitz. Walker's a pain in the butt, not a killer."

The other shifted his eyes from one to the other of us with the jolly lights still dancing in them. Some mortician was going to have fun trying to jack that smile down from his face. Then he left us, heading for the street.

"Watch him," warned Alderdyce when we were among the familiar men's-room surroundings of his office in the C.I.D. He swung a long leg over the corner of his gray metal desk and began patting his pockets. "He's got Proust's ear, and you know what *he* thinks of you."

My old friend Inspector Proust. I wondered if he was still notching the grip of his pearl-handled Colt automatic. I dug out my pack of Winstons and offered one to John. "Nobody can accuse me of sucking up to the brass," I said, lighting his and then mine. It tasted good on my empty stomach. Like sucking a tire. "What about Fitzroy's partner?"

"Cranmer? He's a psycho. One of the little side benefits of lowering the standards to achieve racial balance in the police department."

I watched him smoke. "I thought you quit."

He made a face, drawing on the butt. "Don't you start on me too. I get enough of that from my wife. That's no pool cue between your fingers."

"If I had to give up everything that could kill me, I'd commit suicide. What about the slug?" I sat down on a hard chair. Compared to the one in the interrogation room it was a hassock.

He thrust a hand into his side pocket, brought it out, and uncurled it beneath my nose. Against the dusty pink of his palm it looked tiny and insignificant, hardly lethal. Bits of lint adhered to the snarled lead.

"A thirty-two," he explained, "probably fired from a revolver, on account of no jacketing. Also there was no casing left behind. The M.E. pried the slug out of Jefferson's spine, where it lodged after piercing his right lung.

19

Death occurred around two A.M. He drowned in his own blood, by the way."

I nodded, just to be doing something. "Angle?"

"Straight on."

"That would make the killer about Jefferson's height."

"The hell. Guns are portable; that's why they call them handguns. It could have been a midget standing on a chair. Or Jefferson could have been on his knees, saying his nightly prayers. You've been reading Sherlock Holmes again."

"It helps me forget my work." I clamped the cigarette between my teeth and turned my attention toward making myself presentable. He watched me.

"You want to tell me about your client?"

I related my brief interview with Ann Maringer, leaving out the part about the diamond ring. I didn't know why. Repeating it, I understood why Fitzroy hadn't bought my story. I was having trouble with it myself. "The rest you know," I concluded, "or should. It's on the tape."

"She didn't say why she was expecting to disappear?"

"That was to come later. How was I to know there wouldn't be one?" I did up the necktie, suppressing the urge to check my reflection in John's bald spot. My neck felt like an emery board.

"How much retainer she give you?"

"She didn't, and if she had it wouldn't be any of your business."

"Murder is my business."

"I read that book," I said. "Anyway, it isn't your case."

"Don't remind me. Half the department's on hold waiting for all hell to break loose with the Steelhaulers. They take me off Homicide to brush up on crowd control, and when something happens that might trigger violence, who gets it? Harold Evan Fitzroy, who, when asked during training the best way of preventing a civil disturbance, replied that it was a tossup between riot guns and tear gas." He spat smoke bitterly and snapped away his butt to join the others on the dirty linoleum.

"You should air your feelings," I cautioned. "You'll get ulcers."

"Listen to the virus talk about cold prevention."

"Is there going to be a ruckus?"

He started counting on his fingers. "The rank and file is talking strike. The union brass is talking wait and see. The steel mills are hiring scab labor in case the drivers go out. Every gun shop in town has ammunition on reorder. So far every effort to avoid a ruckus has been spared."

"What do the drivers want?"

"What do I look like, a fucking shop steward? Quit changing the subject! You never did anything for nothing in your life. Why should you start with this Maringer woman?"

"I think it was her eyes," I said.

"Is that what you call them?" He hurried on before I could figure out what that meant. "What makes you think your client didn't kill Jefferson and blow?"

"Every time I wash it that way the colors run. If she left on her own, why didn't she take her purse? Her bank book showed enough cash to get her out of the state and then some. Besides, I tossed her place and didn't find the peekaboo costume she'd had on earlier. How far would she get dressed like that?"

"Don't try to butter me up by feeding me straight lines. She could have changed at the cellar joint, or maybe she threw something on over the costume."

"She kept the place pretty neat, except for the clothes I figure she was wearing before she changed into the costume, slung over the end of the bed. So what would she have to change into at the bar? And if she was in such a hurry that she didn't bother to shuck the costume, why wouldn't she have just grabbed them instead of something harder to get in a drawer? And even if you answer those questions there's still the abandoned purse. It's all circumstantial, but it piles up."

"At this time of year she'll freeze to death."

"She's wearing a coat, if the empty hanger in her closet is any indication. And that's not the only thing missing." I

21

waited for him to ask. When he didn't, I continued. "There wasn't a single photograph in the apartment. Not of her, not of anyone else. She didn't even have a driver's license in her wallet. That didn't seem to bother Fitzroy. Okay, so maybe she's camera shy. But what about family, friends? You don't normally give up things like that unless the alternative is pretty grim. That would be one reason for her not having any ID, or at least one that meant anything. Anyone can take out a savings account under any name."

"You think she was hiding from something?"

"Or somebody. Which could explain why the killer took her along instead of just offing her on the spot." I got up and crushed what was left of my cigarette beneath my heel. It was seven-thirty and I felt like an open sore.

Alderdyce said, "I don't imagine it will do any good to tell you to hang back on this one."

"Has it ever?"

"Why? There's no percentage in it."

"I've been hired to do a job. I'll try to stay out of the cops' way, for what it's worth."

"The road to hell is smooth as glass, Walker. It doesn't need your help." He made out a release order for my car, which had been impounded, and handed it to me.

I put on my coat and hat. "Just so I can say I asked, did Bingo Jefferson have any enemies besides the Mafia and the steel mills?"

He hefted the metropolitan telephone directory from his desk, six pounds of paper and ink made flabby with use. "If you've got a couple of minutes, I'll cross out the names that don't apply."

I grinned. "Get some sleep, John. You spend too much time at the station." I stepped out and got the door shut just as the directory thudded against the pebbled glass.

4

My little one-bedroom house in Hamtramck accepted my return with the glum indifference of an old dog that had long since given up on receiving affection. The air was stale, and dust swirled in the sunlight slanting in through the windows. I showered off the smell of cops, fixed myself a drink, and sipped it between scrapes of my razor. It made my hand steadier, so I left the razor soaking while I fixed another. I spent most of the morning wearing toilet paper on my face.

Robed and carrying my drink, I went into the kitchen, made coffee and a fried egg sandwich, and ate it sitting in the nook as I paged through the morning edition of the *News,* which I had picked up on my way home. Bingo Jefferson's misfortune, reported just before press time, was disposed of in three paragraphs on an inside page under the heading MONTANA BODY GUARD FOUND SLAIN. The location was referred to simply as "an apartment on Cass," and a suspect was reported in custody. Me, though they didn't use my name. There was no mention of Ann Maringer.

I was too keyed up to sleep. I grabbed a broom and a dust rag and put my three rooms and bath to rights, then flipped on the tube, where the earlybird movie was just winding up. *Background to Danger,* with George Raft. A wartime propaganda piece, in which the Americans were the good guys and our battles were fought two thousand miles away by hired men in uniforms that helped you separate friend from enemy. I like old movies; my ex-wife used to say that I liked them more than her. She was right. They're a yardstick for determining how far we've come or how much ground we've lost. In this case I couldn't decide which it was. I turned off the set in the middle of a commercial pitch for the "Hits of the Dave Clark Five" and went to bed.

After a couple of hours of rest without sleep I got up ahead of the alarm, knocked off a hundred pushups just to prove I could, put on my good suit and a tie I hadn't got around to wearing yet. If I didn't feel like a new man I could at least look like one. My heap started with the indignant noises a horse makes when it thinks it deserves a rest, but on the road the mammoth transplanted Cadillac engine took over and conveyed me in satisfactory time to the east side. It was a sunny day and the hookers were in full bloom.

I touched all the bases. The landlady at the apartment house, black and tart-tongued, with harsh creased features and a voice like a boat whistle, said she'd spoken to all the cops she cared to for one day and tried to bang my face with her door. I pried myself in with a roadwise five-dollar bill long enough to learn that her dancing tenant had been living there for only six weeks, that she always paid her rent on time, and that the landlady made it a point never to pry into her lodgers' business. I left while she was telling me a funny story about the two queens who were living together on the top floor. I used the pay telephone outside her door to dial the number I had in my notepad for Nate Washington, who my client had said had referred her to me. A recording informed me that it was no longer in service. On the lam, I thought as I hung up and retrieved my dimes.

A black in dirty green work clothes was sweeping curls of dust across the sky-blue floor of The Crescent as I descended the steps and asked him if the owner was in. He wagged his head toward an open door behind the bar.

The man in the storeroom was an Arab, tall and thin, with a beak nose and Valentino eyes. He had lobeless ears very flat to his head and black hair that gleamed blue in the dim overhead light. His suit was new, the crease on the trousers as sharp as the edge of a fresh hundred-dollar bill. He was watching a pair of men, one black and one white, check off the names on the labels of bottles in wooden cases against a list on a clipboard in the black man's hands as I approached.

"More police?" he asked, after I had introduced myself and explained the nature of my visit. His intonation rose and fell monotonously, like a chant. But his English was good. "No wonder I pay such taxes."

"I'm not with the police. I've been hired to find Ann Maringer. What can you tell me about her?"

"She was a good dancer."

I waited, but he didn't add anything. "That's it?"

He shrugged exaggeratedly. "How much more must one know to hire a dancer? Nothing else is any of my business."

"How long has she worked here?"

"Since February. I have told the police this."

"What about Bingo Jefferson, the dead waiter? When did you hire him?"

"I didn't."

"Who did?"

"No one."

I said, "You mean he just started working? Just like that?"

"Not quite. He came to me last night just before opening. He said his name was Ben Adams and that he was filling in for my regular waiter, who was sick. Franklin Detwiler."

"Where can I reach him?"

"He lives with Coral Anthony, one of the dancers."

"You mean she lives with him?"

"If that was what I meant I would have said that. What's that wet there? Open that case." He indicated a sealed crate atop a stack in the corner, dripping with moisture. The white worker took up a crowbar and inserted it between the boards on top. Nails shrieked as he applied leverage.

"Where can I reach her?" I shouted, over the din.

"Who?" The Arab was concentrating on the crowbar's progress.

"Coral Anthony. The dancer Detwiler lives with."

"Look her up. Can't you see I am busy?"

I waited while the loose board was pried off and the three inspected the crate's contents. Then: "Did Jefferson have his baseball bat with him when he came on?"

The Arab looked at me strangely. His sharp, desert-brown features were dominated by large black eyes like dates, lusterless, without moisture. "I know you," he said at length. "I saw you talking to Ann last night. You are the man who attacked my waiter."

The two workers turned to stare at me. I was vaguely aware that the janitor's broom had stopped sweeping outside the storeroom. Tension grew like mushrooms in the damp.

The Arab said, "Grab him."

The black man dropped his clipboard clattering to the cement floor, took the crowbar from his partner's hands, and came toward me, jiggling it. He had thick, sloping shoulders and a head of close-cropped grizzled hair mounted on a short neck. The light from a dusty fifty-watt bulb in the ceiling shone purple off a scar like a dueler's cicatrix on his glistening brown cheek. I seized a bottle by the neck from a nearby crate and smashed it against the edge. The jagged end glittered in my hand. Whiskey fumes—rank, nauseating in that close room—enveloped me.

My challenger hesitated a moment, then grinned. He liked the idea. We were squaring off when the Arab swept a short-barreled revolver out of his expensive jacket and showed me the round blue emptiness of its bore.

"Please release the bottle." To the man with the crowbar: "I said grab him, not fight him."

My weapon tinkled against the concrete floor. Immediately the gun swung in a short, vicious arc and caught me on the side of the head. Purple lights blossomed behind my eyes. I staggered backward, coming up hard against a stack of crates behind me.

"I think that the police will be interested in the package we have for them," he announced calmly, transferring the

26

revolver to his other hand and shaking circulation back into its mate. "But not until we have finished with him."

"You're finished."

I recognized the voice, its flat blandness, but I was too busy marshaling my senses to place it right away. The Arab turned toward the door, through which Lieutenant Fitzroy was striding. His expression beneath the porkpie hat belonged to someone who had just remembered a wry joke.

"Lieutenant," greeted the owner, his tone drenched with Near Eastern hospitality. "I was just going to call the station. We have your murderer."

"I hope you also have a permit to carry that, Mr. Krim."

The Arab glanced down at the gun as if he'd forgotten he was still holding it. "Of course."

"I see it's a thirty-two caliber. Would you object to our borrowing it for a comparison test?"

"Not at all." His teeth glowed against the brown of his skin. "If you have a warrant."

Fitzroy smiled back. They were fast friends, these two. Krim put away the revolver.

"Hello, Mack," said the lieutenant to Scarface. "Glad to see you learning some trade besides making license plates."

Mack, still holding the crowbar, grumbled something I didn't catch and dropped it. It clanged deafeningly.

Fitzroy said, "Walker has already been in custody and released for lack of evidence. If you'd excuse us I'd like some time alone with him."

The Arab's eyes, almost without whites, shifted from my face to Fitzroy's and back to mine. Finally he nodded. "Fortunately we do not require evidence."

"Thank you," said the lieutenant, as the workers followed their employer out the door. "This city could do with more public-spirited citizens like yourselves." He watched as the door closed. Then he whirled and sank a fist in my stomach. I doubled over, emptying my lungs.

"Just a little reminder to stay out of my case," he explained. "The landlady at the apartment house called me after you left. I figured you'd come here next. You're as

27

predictable as you are curious, Walker. Sooner or later one of them's going to get you killed.''

I took a deep breath and let it out slowly to easy the pressure. "Thanks for the advice, Lieutenant." My croak was fairly normal. "I won't forget it."

"Are you threatening a police officer?"

"I wouldn't dream of it. But if you hit me again you'd better have a month's sick leave built up."

He watched me closely. "I'm strongly tempted. I'd like to see how much of you is mouth and how much muscle."

"Screw you, Lieutenant."

Seeing his jaw tighten and his muscles bunch, I braced myself. I'd promised him one more try; after that things were going to get lively. Then he relaxed, smiling.

"Some other time, shamus," he said. "When there are no witnesses around to tell the judge the big mean cop beat up the defenseless snooper. Yeah. I'd really like to see."

"Where's Tonto?"

"If you mean Sergeant Cranmer, he's doing some leg-work for me. I didn't know you were a racist."

"Goons come in all colors. You're a prime example of that."

"I should be offended," he said cheerfully. "I'm not. I asked around about you. Stackpole at the *News* says if you ever murdered anyone you'd probably have a good reason. Alderdyce doesn't like you much, but he says your word is good, eventually. He claims you're a good cook and that you like old movies."

"Not all old movies," I put in. "Just some. And I don't get as much chance to cook my own meals as I used to."

"Who gives a damn? You fought in Nam, played cop in the army, took a stab at the police training course here, and dropped out. Why you dropped out is none of my business. The point is, the worst anyone has to say about you is that your mouth is faster than your brains, which I knew going in. Maybe you didn't kill Jefferson. Maybe you're just doing your job, like me. But you're grubby, Walker. You follow a grubby line of work, snooping for grubby people. You know what a grub is? A slimy gray

28

worm that steals food in the dark and shrivels to nothing when the sun shines on it.''

"Don't be cagey, Lieutenant. You don't like me.''

"You're starting to shrivel,'' he observed. "Right before my eyes.''

"I'm just doing my job, like you said.''

"Back off, grub. Otherwise I'll leak your name to the press as a suspect in the Jefferson murder and you'll be grouse for every black militant in town, not to mention Phil Montana.'' He pulled open the door. "You go first. Arabs hold grudges and I don't want two murders on this street the same day.''

THE TELEPHONE DIRECTORY HAD CORAL ANTHONY LIVING on Brainard. It was a solid old structure with an ornate façade blurred with age and a frieze of colored glass across the front, those pieces that remained in place catching the light and throwing it back among the blank spots like the sparkle in a dirty old man's eye. The dancer's name stood alone in neatly printed capitals on a yellow slip of paper taped next to the room number in the foyer. The main door was unlocked. I went on up.

"Who is it?'' drawled a feminine voice in reply to my knock.

I gave her my name and added: "I'm pushing my card under your door.''

Halfway through, the card darted from under my propelling finger. I rose.

"What do you want?''

"I'm investigating Ann Maringer's disappearance,'' I said. "I'd like to ask you a couple of questions.''

Locks and chains rattled, a lot of them. Finally the door opened about eight inches and I was confronted with a striking aquiline face the color of old gold. She had high cheekbones and large dark eyes with hard black lashes like curry combs and cornrowed hair and a long neck that swept in an uninterrupted line to the division of her breasts, framed in heart shape by the lapels of a red velour robe growing shiny in places. She was nearly as tall as I am. I

29

glanced down and glimpsed golden toes peeping out of flat-heeled slippers. The trip back up to her face was scenic, as the robe clung to her various hills and valleys like a very thin coat of red paint.

She said, "Like I told the cops, I don't know nothing about her. She was too stuck up to associate with the likes of us pore niggers."

"I caught your act last night," I said. "You dance like a muleskinner's whip."

"Is that a shot or what?"

"More like what. I said it to keep you from slamming the door. But I do like the way you move."

"You lose." She started to push the door shut. I leaned against it. Her eyes grew hard, not that they had been soft before.

"A cop lives in this building. You want me to scream rape?"

I let my eyes wander past her shoulder. A suitcase lay open on a shabby overstuffed chair behind her, half full of clothing. "Going somewhere?"

She filled her lungs. I withdrew my shoulder. She hurled the door shut with a noise like a train crash. Locks snapped, chains jingled.

Moving casually, I descended the stairs and rounded the corner to where I'd left my car, fired up a weed, and drove around to the front of the building, where I parked across the mouth of an alley and sat there with the engine running, smoking, waiting. I turned on the radio and listened to the noon news. The President was vacationing in California. Eleven United Steelhaulers' members were on their way to jail after rioting outside the Renaissance Center, where Phil Montana kept his headquarters, that morning. The cold front was heading south. The Pistons were on a jet to L.A. to take on the Lakers. Everyone was going somewhere but me. There was no mention of the Jefferson killing. I turned it off and sat waiting, smoking.

A Checker cab stopped in front of the building and blew its horn. I took one last drag and screwed out the butt in the dashboard ashtray. She came out a minute later, wearing a long coat and boots and a hat like Ingrid Bergman wore in *Casablanca* and lugging the suitcase. The driver got out and manhandled the case into the trunk, opened the rear door for her, climbed back under the wheel, and spun rubber getting away from the curb. I gave him a block before pulling out to follow.

On Woodward I thought he'd made me. The third time he checked his rearview mirror I fell back and swung east on Warren, then burned up the pavement on John R getting back. Then I hung a left onto Kirby and stopped at Woodward just as he was cruising past. I flipped down my visor to keep his passenger from getting a good look at me and hoped he wouldn't recognize the car.

By this time I had a fair idea of their destination. I took my time easing into the northbound lane and was two blocks back when they hit the west ramp of the Edsel Ford. Traffic on the expressway was heavy; I managed to lose myself in the press of vehicles for the half hour it took us to get to Detroit Metropolitan Airport. At American Airlines I parked in a space for the handicapped while the cabbie was unloading her suitcase in front of the terminal, watched as he pulled away, and legged it to catch up with her in the crowd.

A voice like the oxygen feed in a fish tank announced over the P.A. that American Flight 527 to Los Angeles was now boarding at Gate 17. That's when I spotted her, moving along with the line toward said gate, arm in arm with a tall black man who I'd have bet Ann Maringer's diamond ring answered to Franklin Detwiler.

I was trotting in that direction when Lieutenant Fitzroy's partner Sergeant Cranmer stepped out of a group clustered around the security arch, flanked by a pair of uniformed officers, flashed his badge, and took the couple away without even giving them a chance to reclaim their luggage.

5

I GOT BACK TO MY CAR JUST AS A BIG COP WAS COMING UP the aisle wrestling his citation pad out of his hip pocket. He stood chewing gum and watching me through the blank lenses of his dark glasses as I pulled out. I was making myself very popular with the authorities today.

No one was waiting to take advantage of my considerable services as I walked through the shallow outer room to my office and unlocked the door. The blinds were drawn, casting a gray haze over the desk and filing cabinets that came with the rent, the telephone that rang only when I wasn't there, the safe my late partner had bought to store valuables in and that usually contained my laundry, and the general appearance of competition the Pinkertons didn't lose much sleep over. So much of the lettering. A. WALKER INVESTIGATIONS had flaked off the outer door that the pebbled glass looked like a flea's dance chart. It wasn't much better with the lights on, but it was where I made my living, or tried to.

"You May Have Already Won," gushed the only letter in the slot. I laughed nastily and flipped it into the green metal wastebasket on my way to the desk. Sitting down, I dialed my answering service and asked if there were any messages. Just one, from my ex-wife, reminding me that this month's alimony payment was past due.

"Were those her exact words?" I asked the female voice on the other end.

"I'm sorry, Mr. Walker, but FCC regulations forbid me to quote the message verbatim."

I hung up, unwrapped the taco I had invested in on my way across town, and was about to bite into it when some of the sauce dribbled onto my palm and I remembered Bingo Jefferson's blood on Ann Maringer's carpet. I rewrapped it with the circular. I opened the deep file drawer, got out the fifth of Hiram Walker's—not even a distant cousin—stood it up on the desk and stared at if for a while, then put it back and closed the drawer. Nothing seemed good.

Information gave me the number of United Steelhaulers' executive offices in the Renaissance Center. I got a busy signal, depressed the plunger, and tried again. It rang twice and was answered by a cool, self-assured, masculine voice that sounded as if its owner had been expecting me to call just that time. It recited the number I had just dialed. Somewhere in the background an orchestra nobody had ever heard of was playing "Feelings." These days every office sounds like a cheap nightclub.

"I'd like to speak to Mr. Montana," I said.

"May I ask what about?"

"You may if your name is Mr. Montana."

"Your name, sir?" The temperature went down a degree.

"Walker."

He repeated it. I half expected him to spell it next. When he didn't I said, "That's right. Is he in?"

"Mr. Montana is a busy man, Mr. Walker. I'll have to know your business."

"I'm investigating the Bingo Jefferson murder. I'd like to discuss it with him."

"I see." It didn't sound as if he did. "Are you with the police?"

"Not exactly."

"You mean not at all."

I was elated. I bet no one had gotten his goat in a long time. In the background the taped orchestra paused briefly, then struck up a lively rendition of "Raindrops Keep Falling on My Head." I said, "I'm a private investigator. Jefferson's death is connected with a case I'm working on. Now may I speak to him?"

"Mr. Montana has already discussed that matter with the police. He has nothing more to say."

"I might believe that if you'd ask him."

"I am Mr. Montana's personal secretary. I speak for him."

"Is that all you do for him?"

"That means what?" The viciousness of the retort made me withdraw the receiver from my ear. It was like a brief glimpse at something he preferred to keep hidden, like an insane brother locked in the attic. I backed water.

"Just making conversation. How long can it take to ask you boss if he wants to talk to me? You can put me on hold. Just don't turn on any more music."

"I am Mr. Montana's personal secretary," he repeated coldly. "One of my duties is to screen his calls. I'm sorry, but he's far too busy. And so am I. Good-bye."

It was the nicest way I had ever been hung up on. I pressed down the plunger again and dialed the number for the third time. After two rings the same cool voice came on again. I got a picture of him sitting at his desk and counting them. The orchestra was still playing "Raindrops."

"I'd like to speak to Mr. Montana."

There was a pause, then: "Listen, Jack, I don't know what your game is, but Phil Montana is no man to play it with." His tone was guarded. His earlier lapse had sharpened up his defenses.

"I thought I might catch you in a better mood." I was speaking into a dead line. This time he hadn't been nearly so polite about it.

I replaced the receiver and stared at it for a while. Casting around for something to do next, my eyes fell to the chipped safe.

The diamond, unconcerned by its tawdry surroundings, winked coquettishly in the overhead light as I turned it over between my fingers. Still holding it, I went over to the only drawer of my filing cabinet that contained anything, unlocked it, and drew out a little book with a red plastic cover. I found Mike Pilaster's number written in my special code and put the telephone back to work. The receiver was still warm from the last time. I lit a cigarette while it was ringing.

It rang fourteen times. Anyone who gave up after ten wasn't somebody he wanted to talk to. A hard, bitter voice said, "Yes." That was the way it sounded over the wire. In person it was much less friendly.

"I have an item on which your opinion would be of great value." I didn't use his name, nor did I identify myself. Mike had a photographic ear and a neurosis about electronic listening devices.

"How great?"

"I'll let you decide."

"I'm free at two-thirty." The line clicked and buzzed.

I had to hump it it to get to his junk shop in Southfield by the appointed time, stopping off at my bank to dip into working capital. The shop was located in an ordinary house on Telegraph, a brick colonial with a beautifully landscaped lawn and a sign over the door bearing the legend *Curiosities* in elegant script. The interior was jammed with tables supporting lamps, antique clocks, old farm tools, porcelain figures, fixtures, books in every conceivable language, boxes of horse tack, ladies' chamber pots decorated with flowers and a gold stripe, powder horns, bottles, clothing, newspapers dating back to the Spanish-American War. Fire hoses, flat and black and cracked with age, lay in coils on the hardwood floor among crates of dusty piano rolls and steam wrenches of Brobdingnagian proportions, once used to maintain mining machinery in the Upper Peninsula. Plows and saddles hung from the ceiling. On the far wall was mounted a stoic-looking moose head that might have been shot by Teddy Roosevelt before he went to Washington, its eight-foot rack strung with uniforms from all sides of the First World War. In the center of all this stood a doughnut-shaped wooden counter, itself an antique, where a thin, steely-haired woman in rhinestone-rimmed glasses and a blue business suit was haggling with the man behind the counter over the price of a square mantel clock with a gilt cupid perched on top. The place smelled of musty old leather.

"Eighty dollars it is, Mrs. Crepps." The merchant, a short, elderly party in a loud vest, with a mop of gray hair going white on one side, sounded surly as he rang up the purchase on a cash register almost as old as he was. "Sometimes I wonder if this hobby is worth the expense."

The lady laughed and counted out four twenties from a clutch purse that matched her suit. "I'll let you in on a little secret, Mr. Pilaster," she said. "I've been looking for this particular piece for ten years. I'd have gone as high as a hundred and fifty."

"Congratulations. Now get out of my store."

She passed me on her way out, carrying her treasure unwrapped beneath one arm and laughing. When she was gone I said, "Sounds like you're slipping, Mike."

"I'll let you in on a little secret, Walker." His sour, seamed face gave no indication that he realized he was mimicking his late customer. "There's no sucker like a sucker who fancies himself an expert." From under the counter he hoisted another mantel clock exactly like the one he had just sold, opened the counter flap, and stood the item in an empty spot on a nearby table. Then he went over and snapped the lock on the door and turned the sign in the curtained window around so that it read CLOSED. "Let's go upstairs."

I followed him, almost tripping over a burlap sack full of horse bones at the base of a roped-off staircase. A piece of masking tape stuck to the exposed jaw bone announced in black Magic Marker capitals that it had been sold.

The second floor contained almost as much merchandise as the shop proper, but here it was kept in tall glass cases and ran toward jewelry and firearms, most of it stolen and bought from the thieves for pennies on the dollar. When it

36

came to fencing, Mike Pilaster was an institution. His rap sheet was as long as his leg and went back to 1942. That it included only one conviction, and that one minor, said something for his connections in the City-County Building. He had things in that room I hadn't seen since the last Tet offensive.

"Did you ever get around to having a burglar alarm installed up here?" I hung back to keep from walking on his heels as he waddled on arthritic legs toward a linoleum-topped workbench at the rear of the long room. The floor was carpeted in deep pile the color of old blood. I thought of Bingo Jefferson.

"Where would they sell the stuff?" He snapped on a folding desk lamp, impaling the counter with a hard white beam.

"There's a thought," I said.

He climbed onto a high stool and stared at me with eyes like cracks in a yellow sheet. I drew out my folded handkerchief, peeled it open carefully, plucked out the ring, and placed it in his outstretched palm. He put it down under the lamp's glare with that indifference bordering on contempt shared by all craftsmen regarding the objects of their trade, donned a pair of half-glasses with a jeweler's eyepiece attached, flipped that down, took up the ring, and studied it for the better part of a second. Then he laid it back down and peeled off the glasses.

"It's a diamond," he said.

"That'll settle the argument. The guy in the delicatessen said it was a ham sandwich." I slid a cigarette between my lips. "Can you put a price tag on it?"

"Please don't smoke. My asthma."

"I wouldn't dream of smoking your asthma. What about it?"

"Is it hot?"

"Brother, it's glowing. But not in the way you think. It's tied in with a murder investigation."

He pursed his lips. They were white from chewing antacid tablets. On top of everything else he had ulcers. "I might go five for it."

37

"Hundred?" He nodded. "The party I got it from said I could get seven-fifty."

"Good luck." He extended it for me to take back. I kept my hands in my pockets.

"I'm not selling it. I just want to know what the ring is worth."

"The ring is worth two thousand."

I raised my eyebrows. "Is this a multiple-choice question? I get to pick which one is right?"

"The diamond is worth five hundred to me. If it's hot I'll have to pry it out of its setting. As a piece it'd bring four times that."

"The setting is that valuable? What's the price of gold today?"

"It's not the gold, it's the workmanship. Look at that tooling. He never did better."

"You know who mounted it?"

He settled back on the stool and cupped his knees in his small, sinewy hands. His gaze was steady. "It's highly possible."

"How high?"

"Fifty."

I whistled. "That's stiff for just a name."

"It's a stiff name."

"I don't have that much on me. I'll mail it to you if I think it's worth it."

"Fine. I'll mail you the name."

I made a face and separated two twenties and a ten from my wallet. In the three years since we'd met—never mind how or why—neither the method nor the outcome of our negotiations ever varied. I always ended up paying what he asked. He folded the bills and put them away without ceremony in the pocket of his noisy vest.

"Chester Wright," he said. "Made and sold jewelry in Madison Heights until he retired a couple of years back. But he keeps his hand in."

"That's worth maybe twenty. Give me change."

"I'm not finished. His work is exclusive. One customer only."

38

I waited.

"Phil Montana."

I thanked him and accepted the return of the ring.

6

A GUY WAS READING THE DIRECTORY IN THE LOBBY WHEN
I got back to my building. I was in too much hurry to tell
him that half the businesses listed there were no longer
operating but as I mounted the sneering old stairs I admired
his sharp tailored suit and topcoat with a quiet check. He
was young and tan and his blond hair had that natural wind-
blown look that only professional hands can achieve. He
looked like Troy Donahue. No one looks like Troy Donahue. I was still in shock.

I got a box of paper clips out of my desk and emptied it
into an envelope. Then I folded my handkerchief small,
inserted it in the box, placed the ring on top of that, and
replaced the lid. Somehow it seemed more respectful. I
snapped a rubber band around the box, tucked one of my
cards beneath that, and slipped it into my overcoat pocket.
Troy wasn't there when I descended. I levered my crate
out of the loading zone in front of the building and high-
balled it to the riverfront.

The brown-and-silver towers of the Renaissance Center
rose from the construction surrounding them like feudal
ruins, afternoon sun striping the 740-foot central turret of
the Detroit Plaza, the world's tallest failing hotel. Near that
site in the year 1701, Cadillac erected a village of stout logs
designed to withstand an Indian siege, and in 1974 history
swung full circle when the city he had founded began work
on a structure impressive enough to discourage rioters and
second-story men. The result is a Xanadu overlooking some

of the poorest real estate in the Northwest Territory. The hotel received its baptism of blood shortly before it opened, when a young woman hurled herself from its summit. It was a bad omen. But while the hotel languishes because the city has no tourist trade, the office complex and shopping center prosper, those who can afford the rates flocking to the security of the Center's glass walls like fugitives from Poe's Red Death. Like Ann Maringer's diamond ring, it's a pretty piece of work, and about as necessary as a Tiffany lamp in a home for the blind.

The air was stuffy and moist with false summer, but sunlight bounced hot and dry off the asphalt of the parking lot while starlings scampered this way and that in a frustrated search for grass. Sawhorses shunted off to one side near the staircase to the entrance and a couple of broken bottles were all that remained of that morning's labor disturbance. A black cop whose afro bulged from under both sides of his uniform cap like Mickey Mouse ears eyed me suspiciously as I passed him.

The tower lobby, indirectly lit and smelling like new lobbies everywhere, of fresh wax and filtered air and plastic shoes on a hot day, was nearly deserted, or it looked that way because it was so big. I took one of the exposed elevators that travel up the outside of the building in glass tubes like mercury in July. Riding in it made me feel like a target. Glancing down toward the parking lot, I noticed a man in a topcoat with a quiet check walking rapidly across the asphalt, scattering starlings before him. Then he disappeared inside the building.

It could have been coincidence. In a city this size there were thousands of topcoats like that. And blond men to wear them. I directed my attention to the cityscape, going gray under an approaching cloudbank, and thought.

The entire thirty-eighth floor was leased by United Steelhaulers. They had come a long way from the pitched battles of the Depression, when the steel mills hired cops to break the strikes by breaking heads and union executives were selected for their skill with blunt instruments. They had come exactly thirty-eight floors.

I stepped off the car into a carpeted octagon with elevators on every side but one, a pair of glass doors behind which a middle-aged black man in light blue uniform, with a face like a squashed cigar, sat at a reception desk. I went on in. Two men occupied black vinyl-upholstered couches reserved for visitors, one on either side of me. They were large and well-dressed and sat with their hands resting on their thighs, watching me. A third stood smoking near the desk: A tall man, very slim, in a tan suit cut with an engraving tool, one hand resting casually in his pocket. He was watching me too.

"This isn't a public floor," the security man informed me. His eyes were pinpoints of light in sharp, weathered creases. "You got an appointment with Mr. Montana?"

I ignored him, focusing my attention on the tall man. "You must be the personal secretary."

He spent some time trying to stare me down. He had tan hair clipped short at the ears and neck and combed in crisp waves. His face was the same shade of tan as his hair and suit, as were his eyes, and between them they showed enough expression to fill ant's eye cup. A gray thread worked its way upward from the end of his cigarette to a ventilator hidden in the ceiling, describing a square, twisting pattern that reminded me of the image on the screen of an oscilloscope.

There was something familiar about him. The something flashed in my memory but was gone before I could grasp it.

"That settles that," he said finally, in the cool, self-assured voice I recognized from the telephone. "Now who are you, and like the man said, do you have an appointment with Mr. Montana?"

"I might have if you had let me speak to him earlier."

It took him a moment to place me, but then he had and rage came to his eyes like a face to a window. I looked past him, through the glass beyond the half wall that separated the reception area from the rest of the offices. Outside, the sky was darkening, not with night but with sudden overcast, washing the streets and buildings in middle-register gray, pierced here and there with spots of yellow light like holes in a bedcurtain. On Woodward an opportunistic neon sign squirted now red, now green, while cars crawled past, towed by beams of light the width of toothpicks. Even in the rarefied air of the RenCen I could feel the pressure building. A storm was on its way.

"We must have had a bad connection," said the secretary. "I told you the man is too busy to speak to you." His voice held a cutting edge.

"That was over the telephone. In person he'll have both hands free and can go on working while we talk. I won't mind."

"Get him out of here."

The two men who had been sitting on the couches rose silently. In their nice suits and James Dean haircuts they might have been college proctors but for their height. One of them wore horn-rimmed glasses. They took up positions on either side of me, with Size Fourteens spread slightly and spadelike hands folded in front of them, looking resigned and patient, like tanks in a motor pool.

I slid my hand inside my overcoat pocket and the world stopped turning.

The secretary's eyes flicked to the pocket and his lips parted, showing a row of caps as alike as cars on an assembly line. I felt rather than saw the Terrible Twins place their hands inside their pockets.

"I'm going after a box," I said. "Just a box."

There was another long pause. Even the smoke leaking from the forgotten cigarette seemed to stand still, forming a question mark in the motionless air. Beyond the glass the city had sunk into a crouch beneath the lowering sky, awaiting the first flash and bang. Then the secretary nodded. A nearly indiscernible gesture, involving only his chin. But there on the thirty-eighth floor it carried the force of an explosion.

"Slowly," he warned.

I eased the box into the open and held it out to him. The two giants returned to parade rest. The man in uniform behind the desk relaxed visibly. He was just window dressing, like the sharp suits and the fancy office.

The secretary read my card, rolled off the rubber band, lifted the lid, and spent some time reading its contents carefully. There was nothing written inside, just the ring. I used the time to wonder where I knew him from. He was young, nearly ten years my junior. The others weren't much older, except for the guard. They wouldn't remember, any more than I would, the sit-down strikes of the thirties or machine gun implacements atop the Ford River Rouge plant or Walter Reuther getting kicked down the steps of the Miller Road overpass. Such things would mean no more to them than the casualty count of the Trojan War. They were part of the new wave of hybrid union employees who perspired in bed with blond file clerks and not over vats of glowing molten steel, dined from china at martini lunches rather than from black tin boxes, and thought a clevice was something a two-hundred-dollar hooker showed when she leaned down to pick up her napkin. I had him pegged, but I still couldn't place him.

When the tan eyes rose to meet mine I bet myself ten dollars what he was going to say next and won.

"An engagement's a serious step. Can't we just go on dating for a while?"

I gave him the deadpan. "I guess you fellows don't get much humor up here."

He didn't like that only half as much as he didn't like not getting a laugh out of the others. "I don't get it," he snarled. "What's this got to do with anything?"

He could have been legitimate. He could have been acting. I didn't care either way. "Take it in to Mr. Montana. He'll know."

"I'm not sure I like a shamus coming up here and telling me what I should do. As a matter of fact, I'm sure I don't."

"Call it a request."

"How do I know you're who you claim you are? Assassins have tried to crack our security before. Let's see some identification."

44

"I'm going for my wallet," I told the men beside me, and reached in to withdraw it with two fingers. The secretary gave the photostat license and sheriff's shield the same attention he'd given the ring. I put away the wallet.

"I thought you said you weren't with the police."

"I used to be a process server. The badge is honorary. It's saved me a beating or two."

"Times change." He stood there tapping the box with his index finger, looking every inch the gangster's right-hand man from *The Big Heat*, then remembered his cigarette and took a last drag before flipping it into a steel dingus attached to the wall. "Wait here," he said, exhaling smoke. A meaningful glance at the duo, and he went through the opening at his back.

"What else?" I was talking to the wall.

7

I MADE A COUPLE OF ATTEMPTS TO STRIKE UP A CONVER-
sation with the guards, but they weren't having any of it.
It was getting darker outside. It wouldn't be long now.

The secretary returned, looking cool and unprovoked. I
looked for the ring. He didn't have it, a good sign.

"I'm stunned," he said. "He'll see you."

I took a step and ran into his palm. His tan eyes snapped
beyond my shoulder, and the bodyguard with the glasses
flicked up my elbows with thumbs like air jets and frisked
me from chest to ankles in less time than it takes to tell it.
My hat was lifted from my head, then replaced. He stepped
away, shaking his head.

"You understand the necessity for precautions," explained
the secretary gravely as he stepped aside to let me pass. His
manners had improved considerably since our first encounter.
I had won an audience with Mr. Montana and was thus entitled to such treatment as was reserved for visiting royalty.
But he didn't have to like it.

"We're both working stiffs." I excavated my pack of
Winstons and offered him one.

He accepted the cigarette and broke it in one hand. His
eyes remained on mine as he cast the mangled paper and
tobacco into the steel ashtray.

"If that's the way you want it." I motioned to him to
lead the way.

We followed the curve of the building for forty feet, past
a dozen or so partitioned offices, each with its own desk

and window overlooking the city and the Detroit River with Windsor on the other side. It reminded me vaguely of the set from an executive comedy of the fifties, in which a chain of cute secretaries squeak, "Good morning, Mr. Whoozis," as the gruff businessman in homburg and carrying the *Wall Street Journal* marches between them. Only there wasn't a cute secretary in the place. The desks were occupied by young men in snug Hughes & Hatchers, tripping away at IBM typewriters and video terminals with all the individuality of soldier ants. A tepid rendition of "Summertime" floated out of a speaker mounted near the ceiling of each cubicle. None of the young men looked up as we walked past.

At length we came to a door next to an uninhabited cell, which I took to belong to the secretary. The door was unmarked. He tapped discreetly, and without waiting for an answer opened it and ushered me inside. The door closed behind me.

The office wasn't very impressive. It wasn't big enough for nine holes of golf and you couldn't see more than half of Ontario through the picture window. Fluorescent lights concealed behind frosted glass panels in the ceiling shone down evenly over deep black pile carpeting, a bar in one corner, an Exercycle opposite that, a combination stereo and television set built into the wall, an executive desk with a glass top, telephone, intercom, standard electronic calculator and a lot of paperwork in baskets, and a dozen chairs upholstered in brown leather lined up against the wall near the door, none of them in the same league as the high-backed swivel behind the desk. The walls, paneled probably in oak, were hung with the kind of prints that people working many stories above the street seem to prefer, of mills and horses and covered bridges and fresh-faced girls in yellow sunbonnets sitting under shade trees with their skirts spread about them. Every detail right out of a cartoon n *Business Week*, with one exception: On a built-in bookshelf behind the desk, a soiled baseball from the 1968 World Series, signed by all the Tigers and looking as out of place as Huck Finn at the Inaugural Ball.

A small, compact man in shirt sleeves who had been standing at the window with his back to me turned suddenly and I saw that he was holding the box I had sent in, still open with the ring exposed. Few Detroiters could fail to recognize the broad, square face and iron-gray hair cut into a military brush that so delighted the cartoonists on the *News* and *Free Press*, or the diminutive but powerful frame of the ex–Golden Gloves champ who had gained nationwide notoriety that September day in 1936 when, as newly elected head of the Detroit local, he led a gang of steelhaulers armed with wrecking bars and wrenches into a bloody melee with strikebreakers not six blocks from where we were standing. In the years since he had been seen haranguing crowds of gibbering truck drivers in newsreels and on television, invoking the Fifth Amendment during Grand Jury probes into union racketeering, and, more recently, in a widely circulated photograph, swamping out a cell block in gray prison garb after his conviction for assault with a deadly weapon.

He had lost his temper and knocked down a minor union official caught with his hands in the till. That would have been the end of it, except Montana's enemies got wind of the incident and someone remembered that the former boxer's fists were still registered as lethal weapons. He was relased after serving eight months of a year's sentence, but it had taken him two years to claw his way back to the top of the union. Every day of that period was recorded in the fresh lines of his face, the set grimness of his broad mouth, the slackening of his jowls that no cartoonist had yet been able to capture.

His pale gray eyes watched me curiously for about a minute. Finally he walked over to the desk and set down the box containing the ring, next to my card, which lay face up on the blotter.

"Amos Walker," he said, looking at me again. "I thought I knew that name. Weren't you in on the Freeman Shanks investigation?"

"Me and everyone else but the Texas Rangers." I wondered where he got his information. As far as the public was concerned the cops had solved the black labor leader's killing all by themselves.

He charged the bar. I was startled by the sudden energy of the maneuver. "Scotch or rye? I don't stock anything else." He scooped a pair of barrel glasses out of the rack.

I asked for Scotch rocks. He nodded as if in approval, clattered two ice cubes into each glass from a bowl of them on the bar, and filled them both from the same bottle. "The bar was Bill's idea," he explained as he handed me my drink. "He said it was better for my image than a bottle in the desk. Maybe so, but it's a hell of a long walk when you're thirsty."

I said something appropriate and sipped. It was twelve-year-old stuff. "Bill?"

"Bill Clendenan. You met him outside."

"Your secretary."

He laughed shortly, a pleasant barking sound. His voice was like fine gravel. "It that what he's calling himself these days? Well, maybe."

I watched him, a hard man in shirt sleeves with striped tie at half-mast and cuffs turned back to expose thick fore-arms matted with black hair going gray. He and the base-ball were two of a kind. Moving quickly, he circled behind the desk and gestured for me to pull up one of the leather-upholstered chairs. The cushions gripped me like a pudgy hand. He sat, drank just enough of his Scotch to keep it from brimming over, grimaced when it struck bottom, and set the remainder down on the glass surface of the desk, where it stayed throughout our interview. No sight is more tragic than that of a man who likes to drink having to coddle a sour stomach. The gray eyes sought mine.

"Where's Janet?"

I had been holding my hat in my hand. I leaned down and placed it on the carpet, straightened, crossed my legs, sipped my drink, and returned his gaze.

"Janet?"

He made another face. "Don't any of you leeches play anything a way it hasn't already been played in the movies? Let's cut right through the bullshit. What is it, ransom or

49

blackmail? Because if it's blackmail I'd just as soon toss you through that window. It doesn't bother me a bit that it doesn't open."

I said, "Let's go back to the overture. Who's Janet?"

He glared at me from under eyebrows that refused to go gray. I glared back. It was like looking at one of those cut-away models at the auto show and seeing the fan turning and the pistons pumping. "Maybe you'd better start with the ring," he said, flicking a finger at the box on his desk. "Where'd you get it and how'd you trace it to me?"

"It was given to me last night as a retainer for a job. I consulted an expert, who recognized the workmanship and said that it was mounted by a jeweler who works exclusively for Phil Montana."

"This expert wouldn't be Mike Pilaster."

I said nothing. He waved it aside.

"What's the job? Who hired you?"

"When you ask them two at a time, do I get a choice or what?"

"Start with who hired you."

"Uh-uh." I sat back and swirled my drink around in the glass, the way Charles Boyer had done in *Conquest*. The way he had done in damn near all his pictures. "Your turn. Who's Janet?"

"Janet Whiting. Maybe you heard of her."

Something stirred at the back of my head. "Keep talking."

"She was in show business, kind of. Until she got hooked up with a guy named Arthur DeLancey. Could be you heard of him too."

I didn't answer. Arthur DeLancey was a very famous federal judge when he took off in a twin-engine plane for a fishing trip to Canada some years ago and never came back. Part of the wreckage was fished out of Lake Superior a few days after the craft was reported missing, but no bodies were ever recovered. I'd heard a couple of other things as well: That he'd been Phil Montana's chief legal adviser until the two had a falling out during the Grand Jury thing. And that Janet Whiting had been DeLancey's constant companion, the most famous great man's mistress since Marion Davies.

"Let me guess," I ventured. "The ring belongs to Janet Whiting."

"DeLancey and I were still friends then," Montana said with a nod. "He had his eye on a Supreme Court appointment, and the publicity about his relationship with Janet was killing him. He proposed, and I had Chester Wright whip up the ring as an engagement present. The papers were notified that he was seeking a divorce from his wife. We broke up soon after that over some bad advice he gave me, and then he was killed in that plane crash."

"I remember you took some heat about that."

He made a disgusted noise. "The only thing they haven't tried to hang around my neck in the last fifteen years is the '67 riots, and I'm sure someone considered even that. It was about that time—the time of the crash, not the riots—that my wife died. You might say Janet and I were kind of thrown together by circumstances."

"Kind of," I reflected.

"It wasn't much of an affair, didn't even last long enough to make the papers. But we parted friends. We kept in touch until I got sucked in on that trumped-up assault charge and I warned her to steer clear or take the risk of being hauled in as a material witness. The press was just beginning to leave her alone after two years. I never heard from her after that, but I fielded a few rumors."

"What kind of rumors?"

It was his turn to sit back. "You can't buy much for a dime these days, Walker."

"I got a call from a dancer at The Crescent," I obliged. "That's a disco joint in a hole on Cass, run by an Arab named Krim. The dancer said her name was Ann Maringer. When I got there she told me she expected to disappear soon and hired me to find her. This made me a tad curious, but before she could say more she got her cue and asked me to meet her at her place after closing. She gave me the ring to keep me interested. By the time I got there she had blown, leaving behind a very untidy stiff. But you know most of this already, since you had Bingo Jefferson keeping an eye on her. As for my involvement, you would have gotten that from the cops.''

"My connections downtown are spotty since I got out," he replied. "I didn't know you were involved until you told me. I assume you're the suspect they had in custody after Jefferson was killed.''

"And I assume that you think Ann Maringer and Janet Whiting cast one shadow between them." I described her, right down to the borrowed blue eyes. He nodded gravely.

"Janet was in trouble. She dropped out of sight last year, about the time DeLancey's heirs started legal proceedings to have him declared legally dead in order to benefit from his will. I had men out looking for her, but nothing turned up until she was seen dancing at The Crescent. I figured she was in Dutch and sent Bingo to look after her until I could get out from under all this strike crap. That was last night. When you showed up with the ring I thought you were in on the snatch and were holding me up.''

"Any idea who killed Jefferson or why the woman vanished?''

"If I had I wouldn't have agreed to see you, ring or no ring.''

"Jefferson tried to mug me for the sparkler," I said. "Why?''

He looked genuinely surprised. "I didn't tell him to do anything like that. It must have been his idea. Did he have his baseball bat?''

"For a while." I drained my glass, placed it on the edge of the desk, got up, and reached down to pick up my hat. I missed the first time. I'd forgotten about not having had lunch. "You've given me a lot of information, and maybe I owe you this." I adjusted the brim. "The money you paid Franklin Detwiler to skip town after he let Jefferson take his place didn't take. He and his girlfriend were picked up by the cops at Metro this afternoon on their way to California. You'd better get ready for visitors.''

He cursed. "They were here once today already. I said I didn't know what Jefferson was doing over there at that time of night. Now I suppose I'll have to throw them the truth.''

"That works sometimes. What sort of heirs?''

He had been brooding. "What? I'm sorry.''

"You mentioned that Judge DeLancey's heirs were maneuvering to have him declared legally dead. What sort of heirs?''

"His wife Leola. A fourteen-carat bitch. One stepson, Jack. Hers from another marriage; I don't remember his last name. He's your age, or maybe a little older. They were living together last I heard. I'll have Bill get you the number. What will you do now?''

"If I can, find Ann Maringer, or Janet Whiting, or whoever. I've only used up one day of my three-day retainer. Which reminds me.'' I picked up the box containing the ring, replaced the lid and the rubber band, and dropped it back into my coat pocket. I hesitated. "It's none of my business. Was the assault charge really trumped-up?''

The lines around his mouth tightened. "Thirty years ago, even twenty, it would never have come to trial. Back then a bust in the nose was something between men. That was before everyone got so concerned with stamping out violence. Television programming is too brutal. War isn't worth fighting. We're breeding a nation of innocents who have forgotten how to make fists. Meanwhile, that tiny percentage that feels no compunction about using violence watches. And waits.''

"I can see you've given this a lot of thought.''

"I had eight long months to do it in,'' he said.

"Some of your supporters seem to hold the same opinion. That was some tussle out in the parking lot this morning.''

He sneered. "Dissidents, they call them. I call them a royal pain in the ass. I'm busy trying to settle our differences with the steel mills reasonably and they're out busting heads. You know what they're so worked up about? Voluntary overtime. Cost of living increases. Money, for chrissake! Forty years ago we fought for survival. This bunch would kill for another coffee break.''

"You went to prison over a money dispute," I reminded him.

"That punk I decked was stealing from the union. No one does that while I'm in charge. Not one Goddamn pencil. What's your fee?"

I picked up his drift finally and told him. He considered.

"I'll double to have Janet back in one piece. And to have the man who murdered my friend and bodyguard."

"No thanks, Mr. Montana." I buttoned my coat. "In this business, a man has to have certain rules. The first is one case, one client. Thanks for the drink." I paused at the door and went back. He looked up at me, gray eyes unblinking. "Do you know anything about a blond guy in a checked coat who's been shadowing me?"

"No. Is there any reason I should?"

"None I can think of. Except that he wasn't following me until after I spoke with your secretary over the telephone."

"I'll have the phones checked out," he said.

"There's that."

Bill Clendenan was sitting at his desk when I came out. His intercom buzzed and Montana told him to give me the surviving DeLanceys' number. He found it in his Rolodex, wrote it out on a three-by-five card, and handed it to me without looking at me or speaking. I thanked him graciously. He said you're welcome and kindly go to hell. The speaker was playing "Give My Regards to Broadway."

The thunderhead was still an ominous mass over the river when I hit the lobby. Despite the filters the air was hot and heavy, like a hand reaching from the darkness to grasp and smother. My ears wanted to pop.

As I rode down in the elevator, I decided that I couldn't blame them.

8

AT GROUND LEVEL I USED A PUBLIC TELEPHONE TO CALL the number Montana's secretary had given me. When no one answered after eleven rings I hung up. Outside, the pressure had stopped building, to hang on the edge of something like a drop on a faucet, quivering but lacking the impetus to plunge. In the country, birds would be flying crazy and ants would be busy erecting dikes around their holes. Farmers would be corraling the livestock. Their wives would be hurrying to get the wash off the line, if any were left who didn't own electric dryers. In the city we sit still and let the people who get paid for it do what has to be done. Like me. I climbed into my car and swung my nose west. There was no sign of my shadow, which meant exactly nothing.

The downtown branch of the Detroit Public Library in Centre Park occupies the site of the only execution under American law to take place in Michigan. The spectacle of wife-murderer Stephen G. Simmons swinging from the end of a rope in the presence of a festive crowd and a lively band on September 24, 1830, led to the abolition of capital punishment sixteen years later. For some reason the executed party was on my mind as I entered the stone building and crossed from old habit to the microfilm room, where they keep the photographed copies of the *News* and *Free Press* going back to their founding.

The *News* carried an impressive spread on Judge Arthur DeLancey the day he was given up for dead. The front page featured pictures of the wreckage of his airplane and of the Judge himself in happier days, looking dignified and concerned in crisp white hair and handsomely creased face inclining to the oriental and a three-piece suit, no carnation. The names of the pilot and aide who were lost with him were mentioned. I didn't recognize them. Inside, two pages were devoted to his controversial career. A photograph showed him whispering into Phil Montana's ear during the Grand Jury investigation. The labor leader had dark hair back then, but DeLancey's was already white. It happens earlier to some of us, as I well knew. Another caught him at Detroit Metropolitan Airport, his coat over one arm and his wife Leola on the other. He looked weary. She, taller and thin as befitted a former fashion model, with graying hair skinned back and clasped behind her neck, was facing the camera with a tight-lipped smile, as warm as a mortician's handshake. The caption said that they had just arrived from a trip out West, where he had spent much of his time fishing and exploring. His reputation as an outdoorsman had been part of his legend.

In a third picture, he was sitting in a restaurant booth with Janet Whiting, the woman responsible for much of the controversy that had surrounded him. I recognized the three-quarter view of the woman I knew as Ann Maringer, looking elegant in a fur stole thrown back on her bare shoulders and a shift that looked as if it had been pieced together from two sheets of muslin and probably ran into three figures. In black and white her eyes lost some of their innocence, but she still resembled a Barbie doll. They were holding hands, which may have explained why he appeared uncomfortable. The picture would have been taken after their affair became common knowledge.

The text dwelt on his rise from part-time truck driver and charter member of United Steelhaulers while attending law school to his appointment to the federal bench, glossing over his brief and rather tepid career as a union mouthpiece. I grew bored with it quickly and switched to the microfilmed *Free Press* account.

This time there was no feature stuff. An exclusive photo

taken the day of the ill-fated flight posed DeLancey, in old clothes, Windbreaker, and peaked cap, in front of the twin-engine Cessna with his aide and the pilot. The former, a pudgy, balding youth named Pelke, appeared to have reached an uneasy truce with his outdoorsman's outfit. The pilot was wiry and capable-looking in a quilted jacket and canvas trousers and appeared familiar. I squinted at his narrow, dark face, at his hooked nose and large black eyes and glossy black hair, read his name, Lee Collins, squinted at his face again, and sat back and wished for a smoke.

If Lee Collins and Krim, the Arab who ran The Crescent, weren't the same man, they were brothers. Either way it was worth looking into.

9

THE NIGHT WAS STILL HOLDING ITS BREATH AS I approached the unmarked entrance to The Crescent. Shadows, emboldened by the evening's youth, clung to the
inside of the niche as if tensed to spring. The joint wasn't
scheduled to open until eight, but a thin blade of light
showed beneath the door. I descended the concrete steps
and tried the handle. It gave.

Fluorescent tubes I hadn't noticed on my last visit caught
the place naked. Beams that looked like heavy old oak by
phony candlelight were painted plywood. Walls that seemed
thirty feet apart during business hours were closer than
twenty, painted blue at the bottom to match the floor and
to add depth. There were ratholes in the corners. Under a
baby spot, bombarded by the shifting glare of an electric
light show, it all came together, but at this stage the estab-
lishment looked like a hooker the morning after.

The storeroom was in back, behind the bar. I threaded
my way between tables the size of smoking stands with
chairs overturned on top of them to the door marked AU-
THORIZED PERSONNEL and pushed it open. My hand was
inside my coat, gripping the unregistered Luger the cops
had failed to find in the secret pocket of the trunk when
they impounded my car. I wasn't going to make the mis-
take of walking into that storeroom unarmed a second time.
It was empty except for the stacks of wooden crates, cob-
webs, and the smells of liquor and rotting wood. All the
broken glass had been swept away.

I closed the door and turned and froze. From behind the bar I could see a shelf containing a corroded metal cigar box, the kind saloonkeepers use to store the nightly receipts before locking them away in a safe. The lid was open and it was empty.

Which added up to zero. Whoever was responsible for banking the cash could have removed it for that purpose and forgotten to close the lid. That's what I told myself as I crept the length of the bar, looking for something to go with the discovery.

I nearly tripped over him. A gate designed to prevent undesirables from sneaking up on the bartender from the other end cast a shadow that concealed everything but his shoe. I stood there for a long moment, breathing air that had suddenly gone foul, though of course there wouldn't be any noticeable stench. Not yet. Then I reached over and swung open the gate. Light poured into the section.

There was blood, a lot of it. It formed a dark brown oval on the scuffed linoleum all around the body, where it had dried hours before. His head was twisted so that its smashed profile, and particularly the bold nose, stood out sharply against the stain. It was spoiled by a clotted dent in the temple, from which black blood and gray matter ran in spidery lines over his cheeks and down his neck into his collar, all but filling the socket from which his one visible eye stared at everything and yet nothing. He didn't look much like Valentino anymore, and it was a shame about his expensive suit. Gingerly I nudged his outthrust leg with my toe. Steel girders should be that stiff.

I glanced around, searching for the weapon, but nothing looked suitable. If one of the bottles on the shelves behind the bar had been used, the floor would be littered with broken glass. The wound wasn't shaped right to have been made by the edge of the cigar box, and anyway the box was neither stained nor damaged. The hell with it. Finding the instrument of destruction is rarely as important as it's made to be in fiction.

If thoughts were actions I was out of there already and not going through his pockets. I wouldn't know that he carried the usual stuff: loose change, a ring containing what looked like a key to a Mercedes among others, a ticket to Saturday's performance at the Fisher, a flat wallet stuffed with fifties and a driver's license made out to Rahman Hassim Ibn Krim. I would be back home typing up résumés to send to personnel managers in shoe stores. If thoughts were actions, there was no way I would still be in that room standing over a murdered corpse when someone came to the front door.

I heard the handle rattling and vaulted back into the storeroom, where I pushed the door almost shut, leaving a crack just wide enough to observe the newcomer. It was the thickset black I had seen pushing a broom on my last visit. Wearing a greasy jacket over his green work suit, his glowering features all but obscured beneath the bill of a soiled cloth cap, he entered in mid-grumble, muttering about the weather and the condition of the streets and the mayor and life in general with the singsong litany of a man who begins bellyaching in the morning and doesn't stop until he's turned out the light to go back to sleep or had his first drink. He was still at it as he drew near the storeroom. I noticed too late that I was sharing quarters with his broom. Releasing the knob gently, I flattened against the wall and pulled out the Luger.

His footsteps stopped suddenly. I waited for them to resume. They didn't. I remembered then that I'd left the gate open at the other end of the bar and that the body was in plain sight of anyone who happened to glance in that direction. He didn't scream or gasp. They don't, in that neighborhood. He stood still for a space, the way I had, and then his crepe soles kissed the floor swiftly going away, toward where his boss lay. I put away the gun and then, easing open the door to keep the hinges from complaining, crept up behind him on the balls of my feet. He was standing with his back to me and his head bowed, ogling the corpse and breathing like an asthmatic. At the last instant he sensed something and began to turn.

I clamped my left arm across his throat and slammed him hard against me while gripping his right wrist with my right hand, wrenching it back and up. He made a single, guttural noise of raw animal fear, a chilling sound. I choked it off.

"I can crush your windpipe or I can splinter your arm like a bamboo pole," I whispered in his ear. I managed to keep from slipping into the North Vietnamese dialect, but just barely. "Do you believe I can do that? Nod if the answer's yes."

He nodded. His neck was sweating and I could smell the corruption of panic. Something solid in his hip pocket was pressing against my pelvis. I asked him if that was what I thought it was. He nodded again.

"Handy. Or do you always carry it?"

He nodded a third time. He gave good hostage, I'll say that for him.

"Man, scratch anyone over twelve this side of Woodward, you'll find a piece." The words tumbled out shallow and breathless, forced out by the pressure of my forearm against his throat. "Ain't you heard? This here's Dodge City."

"Shame on you," I said. "Renaissance and all." In the advertising mirror behind the bar I glimpsed a face I would cross the street to avoid, strained, tight, and leering. I released him, stepped back, and took the Luger from my pocket. "The iron. Slide it along the bar."

It was nothing, an Italian automatic of no particular make stamped out of sheet metal and exported in a hurry before it blew up in someone's face. I picked it up off the polished counter top and sniffed the muzzle. It hadn't been fired recently. The butt was clear of blood and hair. I dropped it into my coat pocket. Between it and the Luger and the diamond ring I was hauling enough metal to sink an ore carrier.

Turning, the janitor recognized me. I read his thoughts: He was calculating the life expectancy of a man who had seen his boss's murderer. Others followed it, thoughts I liked even less.

"I didn't kill him."

He wasn't convinced. I couldn't imagine why not. I broke the magazine out of the Luger and showed it to him.

"See? Loaded. Why skull him when a bullet is so much

61

neater and more certain?'' I shoved the clip back in, just in case he forgot about the one in the chamber. His gaze roamed toward the corpse and back to my eyes, or rather to the bridge of my nose. The whites were dazzling.

"It's noisier, though."

I pointed the muzzle at the floor six feet away and fired. He jumped halfway up the bar. Concrete dust erupted around the fresh hole in the linoleum. I batted away the metallic gray smoke. "I don't hear any sirens, do you?" My voice sounded strange coming on the heels of the nine-millimeter's deafening roar. "You and I both know that one shot isn't going to bring anyone running in this neighborhood. The exact opposite, in fact. So why bash in his head?"

That stopped him for a moment. Then his face lit up. "Maybe you're one of them maniacs."

I sighed. "I could be, but I'm not. Here." I went for my wallet and he almost got down on the floor beside the dead man. I extended one of my cards. He accepted it like Socrates accepted the goblet, gingerly, between thumb and forefinger. "That's my card. Would a murderer give you his card?"

He read it, moving his lips. "You couldn't tell by me," he said then. "I never met one before. That I know of."

"You think I handed him his ticket because of what he was going to do to me today and because you heard him say I killed Bingo Jefferson. You know there's nothing to the last part, because a cop was here and when we left I wasn't wearing handcuffs. And don't hand me any of that crap about white men looking out for each other. No one thinks that anymore, not this far north, not today. As for the other part, what happened here ended in stalemate; I'd have no reason to look for revenge. The fact is I'm here for the same reason you are, to do a job."

He watched me the way a child watches the parent who's told him he's being punished for his own good and that someday he'll be grateful. I stashed the Luger.

"All right, you don't have to believe me. We'll let the cops sort it out later. Here's how it stands. Someone iced your boss not long after I left and tried to make it look like a robbery by emptying the till. Any other time it could have been robbery, but not now, while I'm investigating another murder and he keeps figuring in. Besides, it was someone he knew or he wouldn't have got this close. It's barely possible that you knocked him down. I don't think so or you wouldn't be here now. The one guy who almost never returns to the scene of the crime is the guy responsible. But it could be you know who is, or at least why it was done.''

I left an opening wide enough for him to leap through. He didn't. But he was interested in what I was saying. I approached it from another angle. "How long have you been working here?"

"Couple of months."

"How well did you know him? Was Krim his real name?"

"All I know is his mother was a bitch. Had to be, to have a son like him. Cheapest bastard I ever worked for, and some of the bastards I worked for would make Jack Benny look like Albert Schweitzer."

"How did he sign your paycheck?"

"He didn't. I always got cash."

"Didn't you question that?"

"Why should I? I figured it's my duty as a citizen to help cut down on paperwork at the IRS."

"Patriotic."

"What you expect?" He was scowling. "Last March I get the census. The questions they ask. How many kids did I have before I got married? What color toilet paper I use? Who bangs my wife when I'm at work? The information is confidential. It said. Couple of months later I start getting mail from places I never heard of, trying to sell me stuff I didn't even know what it was. I wonder where they got my name."

I couldn't use any of that. "Did he have a brother or some other close relative that looked a lot like him?"

"Christ, I hope not. One like him is enough."

There was a door at the other end of the bar, marked

PRIVATE. I cocked my head in that direction. "That the office? Got a key?"

He shook his head. He was still thinking about the census.

"Does anyone have a key to the front door?"

"Only Mr. Krim."

"Good. Lock it." I got out the ring I'd taken from the Arab's pocket and went around the bar the long way while he crossed to the steps leading up and out. I whistled at him. At the landing he turned.

I clanked the Luger down on top of the bar. "Don't let me hear that door opening."

He nodded slowly.

I tried the office door, found it locked, and commenced my game of Russian roulette with the keys, meanwhile keeping an eye on the janitor. For a moment he hesitated, his gaze wandering from gun to me and figuring the distance in between. But he was curious too. The lock snapped home decisively.

The fourth key did the trick. Retrieving the automatic, I motioned the janitor to stay back, nudged open the door with my foot, and spread-eagled against the orange-sherbet wall. No bullets followed. I craned my neck around the jamb. The office was deserted. The janitor's sneer tingled between my shoulder blades as I holstered the Luger and stepped inside.

They'd remodeled right past the place, leaving intact the Roaring Twenties décor, down to a desk Brigham Young had tossed out to lighten his wagon on the trek west and a punch-drunk brass cuspidor that for half a century had been used to catch the water from a leak in the waterstained ceiling. Mosquitoes could have bred in the stagnancy. An antique wooden filing cabinet stood in a cobweb-strung corner against the dank stone walls. I tugged at the top handle. It was unlocked, and for good reason. All three drawers were empty, and from the mold inside had been that way for some time. I lifted the inkstained blotter from the desk and found the initials of someone's grandparent in the bland old oak, nothing else. There was nothing under

64

the telephone either, or submerged in a white china mug three-quarters full of cold coffee. The top drawer contained order blanks scrawled over indecipherably in pencil, a lot of rubber bands, and loose paper clips. A pint of rye whiskey, half full, lay in one of the side drawers beside an upended shot glass and a bottle of aspirins. The next drawer down was empty. The bottom drawer wouldn't budge.

I selected a key shorter than the others on the ring and inserted it. The janitor was watching from the other side of the desk. When the lock clicked he caught his breath. He shifted weight impatiently from one foot to the other as I withdrew a flat booklet in a yellowed plastic sleeve and opened it.

It was an account book, drawn on the National Bank of Detroit in the name of The Crescent. It went back to last year, with a balance forward of $16,996.87 from the previous book. There were no withdrawals, but every other month a deposit had been made in the amount of five thousand dollars. The most recent was dated two weeks ago. The Crescent didn't clear that much in six months, much less sixty days.

I had been careful to handle the book with my handkerchief. Now I slid it back into its sleeve, smeared that between my palms, put it back in the drawer and closed and locked it. Then I went around the office using the handkerchief to wipe off everything I'd been near and a few things I hadn't.

"So what'd you find?" asked the janitor as I hustled him out ahead of me and smeared the doorknob on both sides before locking up.

"It's what I didn't find," I lied. "How come there's no safe in the office? I never saw a bar that didn't have one. And what happened to Krim's thirty-two, the one Lieutenant Fitzroy was so interested in?"

"At police headquarters, I guess. Cops come back a half hour after you left, with a warrant for it. He wouldn't have a safe, claimed it was like advertising to a thief. I heard him say it I bet a hundred times. You think he creamed that guy Jefferson?"

"Not with that gun. He wouldn't have been stupid enough to hang onto it. How long has he owned this place?"

He shrugged. "I heard a year."

"You hear a lot for a janitor."

"Just 'cause I'm poor don't mean I'm deaf."

Only a year. That explained why the IRS hadn't gotten around to asking why Krim never paid anyone out of the account. I said, "There's a C-note in it for you if you forget you found me here. Call the cops, report finding the body, but leave me out of it."

His eyes narrowed. "Let's see something up front."

"Right now I'm strapped. I'll catch you later. You've got the hammer. You can always turn me over if I don't come through."

"Yeah, and tell the cops what when they ask how come I didn't do it sooner? I just got off parole, man. If I risk going back inside, it's got to be for something better than some hoojie's cross my heart and hope to die."

"I'll see what I've got." I reached inside my coat pocket. He watched me, licking his lips. In his greed he forgot that I had my wallet in my breast pocket, not on my hip. He was still watching as I drew out a fistful of his Saturday Night Special and clanked it against the side of his head. He said something that didn't sound like any language I was familiar with and his bones dissolved.

I got my arms around his chest under his arms and dragged him into the office. I started to leave, paused, then went back and got out the biggest bill I had, a five, and thrust it into his jacket pocket.

"Something up front," I said. I locked him in and ditched the keys on my way out. His gun went into the sewer.

10

I WAS DRIVING EAST ON ADELAIDE WHEN THE FIRST FAT drops struck the Cutlass's vinyl top with a noise like grasshoppers bounding off a bass drum. Immediately it swelled to a roar, and the cityscape beyond the windshield dissolved as if the artist had lost patience with it and swiped a turpentine-soaked sponge across the canvas. I could sympathize with that.

Lightning blanched the street, then withdrew, thunder pounding its heels. I switched on the wipers, but I might as well have tried to dig a hole in Lake Michigan for all the good it did. A couple of blocks of that and I pulled into a diner to let it blow over while I wrestled a steak.

The place was too well lit for a fugitive from his second murder in less than twenty-four hours. The only other customer was an elderly black man in a dirty raincoat slurping chili at the counter. He could have been a plainclothes cop. I chose a booth and when the waitress showed up ordered a sirloin I knew would bear little resemblance to the juicy red number pictured on the spotted menu, and a glass of beer.

"We don't serve beer." She was a fat girl with a faint moustache, her middle cruelly bisected by an apron string like a strand of piano wire and her brown hair gathered up under a ducky white cap. She looked like the Pillsbury Doughboy in drag.

"Do you serve water?" I asked.

"When they ask for it. These days it costs us."

"Let's be extravagant."

"That mean you want water?"

I said it meant I wanted water. It was the longest conversation I could recall ever having had on the subject. She wrote it down as if she might forget it between here and the counter twelve feet away and waddled off in that direction. I watched the tall thin guy behind the counter slap a hunk of meat the size of a shoe heel onto the griddle, just to make sure he didn't drop it on the way, then killed time while it was cooking by reading the selections on the juke box controls on the wall of the booth. "How Much Is That Doggie in the Window?" was as funky as it got.

Rain belted the plate glass window in gusts, beyond which the street was as black and inscrutable as Krim's dead eyes. Then lightning hurled everything into blinding unreality, catching pedestrians in mid-lope holding folded newspapers over their heads, the women clutching the hems of their skirts as they ran. Thunder set the building shuddering. They had closed down bars that pandered, slapped injunctions on all-night grindhouses and strip joints, thrown up hotels that stood empty, fiddled with the crime statistics, and coerced the local media into ignoring "two-bit" murders for more upbeat news, but they couldn't stop the lightning or the thunder. I wondered what the mayor thought about that, or if he even heard it through the soundproof walls of his brand-new million-dollar office. I wondered what the motorists stranded in the flooded ditches Detroit calls underpasses thought about it. I wondered what had happened to my steak.

When it came, it was underdone and trying to hide under a sprig of parsley that had come over on the *Mayflower*. I considered sending it back, but was reluctant to make a scene in my soon-to-be-wanted state, and in any case I was too tired and too hungry to argue. Red juice trickled onto the plate as I made my first cut, but I forked the chunk into my mouth without hesitation and chewed it and swallowed and managed to keep it down without thinking too much

68

about the stained linoleum behind the bar at The Crescent. I was getting hardboiled as hell.

I had scooped up the last of the starchy mashed potatoes and was washing the glue out of my mouth with water that had come from the inside of a rusty boiler when a cop came in through the glass door.

Looking showroom new in a shining poncho and cellophane-wrapped cap, he lamped the interior of the diner with the kind of eyes that could spot a paper clip in a bushel of straight pins. Despite his drooping moustache he couldn't have been more than twenty-two, but he looked as hard as a chunk of fresh-split maple. His gaze lingered on me for an instant and then he strode up to the counter, leaving a trail of wet boot prints on the waxed floor. I got my heart going again in time to hear him order six hamburgers and four coffees to go from the fat waitress.

"Some kind of party, Dave?" asked the thin man at the griddle. Six fresh patties struck the hot metal, hissing furiously.

"More like a wake." The cop swung a leg over a stool and sat down, his poncho rustling like a sheet of tin. His voice was a pleasant tenor in spite of his surface hardness. "We got a murder down on Cass, a Class D joint. Looks like robbery. The owner caught the guy rifling the till and got himself sapped but good. The guy sapped another one in the office, but that one's still kicking. One of the dancers found them and called us." He shook his head. "I don't know how those dudes in plainclothes do it. The guy's laying there with his brains showing and they send me out for supper."

"All you cops got cast-iron stomachs. This guy in the office doing any talking?" The thin man turned over the patties with a spatula. Grease spattered his white apron.

"They were trying to bring him around when I left. He had a lump on his head like Tibet has a hill called Everest. Lots of cream in one of those, Sue. The lieutenant says he don't like it black."

The waitress finished filling four Styrofoam cups with

steaming yellow-brown liquid from a glass pot and up-ended the cream dispenser into the last. She handled it as if it had grown out of her hand.

"Punks," said the thin man. "Well, it ain't as if he didn't ask for it, running one of them porno joints. It's getting so I can't take the old lady out for a drink anymore without some broad pushing her tits in my face."

"I'm sure that's why they killed him, Charlie," dead-panned the cop. "They'll probably donate the dough to the Women's Decency League."

"Yeah, well, maybe that wouldn't be such a wild idea." Charlie got the hamburgers between buns and laid them on a tray for the waitress to wrap and bag. "This town started going to hell when Henry Ford started paying five bucks a day and brought all them niggers and hillbillies up from down South. No offense, there."

The old black man gave no indication that he'd heard the crack or the disclaimer. He continued slurping.

"Hey, I'm from Ohio," Sue complained.

"That ain't the South."

"It's south of here."

"So's Dearborn, but I wasn't talking about that nei-ther."

"Before my time." The uniform paid the girl for his order and placed the bulging paper sack under one arm. "Thanks, Charlie. You've made a bunch of fat old detectives very gassy."

"Shove it, Dave. Hey, maybe I'll see all this on the eleven o'clock news."

"The day I marry Dolly Parton."

I watched the cop leave. Lightning limned him briefly as he folded his lanky frame into his scout car out front, then it was dark again until his lights came on and he swung back onto Adelaide. He had no partner. The mayor was cutting back again; I'd heard he was stocking domestic in the wine cellar of his limousine.

"It is too the South," grumbled the waitress. "Ain't you ever noticed my accent?"

"Get your accent over there and give that guy his bill."

70

She did as directed, tearing it savagely from her pad and flinging it down onto my table. I paid at the register, got a quarter in change, and dropped it into the pay telephone near the door. The instrument had been there a while and no one had gotten around to tell Ma Bell that this one was still enclosed in a booth so she could send someone to rip it out. I pulled the door shut and dialed the number Phil Montana had given me. When a Spanish accent answered I asked for Mrs. DeLancey. The maid or whoever it was asked who was calling. I told her, adding where I had obtained the number. I was instructed to hold on.

Two minutes of silence followed. In homes where rich people live you never overhear loud conversations or children galloping up- and downstairs or televisions playing or pork chops sizzling in the kitchen. While I was waiting, the guy in the raincoat finished his chili finally and paid for it and left, walking the way he ate, slowly and deliberately, as if each step counted. If he was a cop he wasn't on Fitzroy's detail.

A woman's voice said, "Leola DeLancey." It was a smooth contralto, totally ageless. It wouldn't have sounded any different ten years ago and would sound the same ten years from now.

"Mrs. DeLancey, my name is Amos Walker." Another thing about rich people is that they expect you to introduce yourself all over again as if the information you gave the maid or whoever hasn't reached them. "I'm a private investigator, looking into the disappearance of a woman who calls herself Ann Maringer. I found a man murdered in her apartment, who led me to Phil Montana, who gave me your number. I'd like to come over and talk."

She had listened in silence. After a couple of seconds of dead air: "I'm sorry, Mr. Walker, but I don't know anyone named Maringer and in any case I'm much too busy to talk to you. I'm afraid Mr. Montana pointed you in the wrong direction. Which doesn't surprise me. Goodbye."

"Her real name was Janet Whiting."

71

I caught her just as the receiver was leaving her ear. For a moment we both listened to each other's breathing. Through the glass of the booth I watch the fat waitress clearing my table and looking for her tip. She'd look a long time.

"Perhaps I could speak with your son," I suggested.

"That won't be necessary," said Mrs. DeLancey. "Neither of us has had any business with Miss Whiting since my husband's death. I really don't see how we could be of service to your investigation."

"It's a murder case now, Mrs. DeLancey. Through no fault of mine or theirs I happen to be a half-step ahead of the police on this one. Sooner or later they'll come to see you, and then you'll be forced to answer some questions. I'm betting on sooner. If you speak to me first, you'll have an idea of what they'll be asking."

"So that I can prepare my answers. Is that what you're suggesting?" Her tone would grow icicles.

"That's up to you, Mrs. DeLancey."

"Would tomorrow morning at nine be suitable?"

"Eminently."

She gave me directions to her house in Grosse Pointe and hung up without saying good-bye this time.

It was still coming down in five-gallon drums when I pulled out of the playing-card-size parking area. My headlamps glared off pavement as wet and black as fresh oil. I turned on the radio in the middle of an emergency bulletin. Funnel clouds had been spotted in Wayne, Oakland, and Macomb counties, and one had touched down in Monroe and turned someone's barn into kindling. I turned it off. No one ever pays attention to those things. The dangers you can count on are problem enough without worrying about something as neurotically unpredictable as a tornado.

I had just time enough to stop at my house, pack a suitcase, and call a cab to take me to a motel. By now the janitor would be talking, and Fitzroy would be putting out an APB on me and my car. All I hoped to gain was a night's sleep and my interview with Mrs. De-Lancey. After that I was theirs.

As I swung into my driveway, my headlamps fell across an unfamiliar brown two-door parked in front of the attached garage. I slammed the Cutlass into reverse, but before the gears could mesh a guy got out from under the wheel of the coupe and stood shielding his eyes against the glare of the lamps.

A blond guy in a checked coat.

11

For no reason other than curiosity I moved the indicator to Park and got out. He stood his ground as I approached. He was medium height, a slice shorter than I, with wide-set eyes the color of morning frost against an even tan, a straight nose, and a jaw that just missed being lantern. He looked like the guy you see in the cigarette ads, romping in the surf with a lush young thing in a bikini and not a cigarette in sight. His hair was sandy when wet, as it was now.

"You've got things backwards, Jack," I told him, gripping the Luger in my coat pocket. *"You're* supposed to be behind *me.* That's the way we've been playing it so far."

"I figured you'd be coming here sooner or later. Before you slug me, read that." He handed me a card he'd been holding cupped in one hand. It was printed in brown characters on heavy pebbled beige stock and read:

RELIANCE INVESTIGATIONS
"Courtesy, Efficiency, Confidentiality"
Albert Gold, Special Operative
Lansing, Mich.

His home number was included in the lower right-hand corner.

"Reliance, huh? I should have known by the smart clothes. All you guys dress alike." I pocketed the card. You never know when they may come in handy.

He nodded. He thought it was a compliment. "You know us, then."

"Five years ago I had a partner. We did some legwork for you on an embezzling case. We ended up going to small claims court to collect."

He nodded again. "It's in the file. Some kind of computer foul-up. Whatever happened to your partner?"

"He died."

"Oh." He looked sad. "Natural causes, I hope."

"Only as far as lead is a natural substance."

"Oh. Can we go inside? I just had a permanent this morning and the guarantee doesn't include a hurricane clause."

"We wouldn't want your mascara running, either."

He flushed under his sun lamp tan. "You're saying what?"

"I'm saying I don't like being followed. I'm saying I don't like people parking on property I pay taxes on, uninvited. I'm saying I don't like glossy detective agencies that hire their talent off a movie lot and drop a bundle on miles of electronic spaghetti and window dressing and base their reputations on the hard work of real investigators not on their payroll and then stiff them. But most of all I'm saying I don't like you."

He bristled. "I ought to punch you out for that. But I won't."

"Aw," I said. "Please?"

For a moment it looked as if he might try it. I was hoping he would. He was all muscle and a thousand dollars' worth of martial arts training, and scraping the driveway with his pretty face was just the release I needed after the day I'd had. But then he seemed to remember the first part of his agency's motto, and relaxed as suddenly as a guard dog upon hearing his master's control word. That's the way it would always work. Let him just entertain the thought of leaning on a reluctant source or acting upon a hunch or trading a small secret for a bigger one, and the credo "Courtesy, Efficiency, Confidentiality" would jerk him back like bait on a line.

75

He said, "If you want me to go I'll go. But I've got a proposition that may prove mutually beneficial if you care to listen."

"Oh, Christ," I groaned. "Not another one."

"What?"

"I've got packing to do. You won't mind if I do it while you talk."

I went back, cut the engine and jerked out the keys, unlocked the front door, turned on the hall light, waved him inside and went back again to kill the headlamps. He was standing in the entranceway trying not to drip on the linoleum. I took his coat, climbed out of mine, and hung them with my hat in the hall closet. I slid the holstered Luger into a more comfortable position on my belt. That bothered him, that did; he almost broke his jaw yawning.

Ditching my jacket and tie on the way to the kitchen, I offered him a drink but he said he was on duty. I said so was I and poured myself a slug from the bottle in the cupboard over the sink and brought it through the living room into the four-by-six bedroom while he tagged along. I tasted my drink, set it down on the nightstand, wrestled my scraped and battered suitcase out of the closet onto the bed, and opened it to let the bats out while I pulled out the top dresser drawer. He watched me from the doorway.

"Going on vacation?"

"Yeah." I placed pajamas and a change of underwear inside the suitcase.

"I'd say you're going on the scout."

I was bent over the drawer pawing through the stuff there in search of a decent shirt. I stopped and turned to face him. He was leaning against the jamb, stroking the guttered paint with a fingertip. It fascinated him. "Spill it," I said. "What are you holding?"

"I followed you to Cass tonight." He poked at the old nail holes where the original owner hung up his dozen kids when they got too frisky. "I was parked outside The Crescent when you came out and looked up and down the street like a Communist spy in a crummy old movie. It made me curious, so I hung around. A girl went in a few minutes

76

later. Pretty soon the police showed up. When they came out and snatched the mike out of the scout car I flipped on my scanner and guess what I heard?''

"The Pistons lost."

"You know what I heard."

I got my pack out of my shirt pocket and shook it. One left. I stuck it in the corner of my mouth and lit it and drew the smoke down deep. It tasted good. I felt good. I had his number. I said, "How much?"

He looked up from the jamb and raised his eyebrows. Montana was right; every one of them spent his evenings in front of The Late Show taking notes. In three strides I was on him and glommed a double handful of his collar. I yanked him into the room and hurled him up against the wall hard enough to knock loose the pictures on the other side. I leaned into him. He wasn't armed.

"I've dealt with every kind of blackmailer and shake-down artist." My cigarette bobbed in his face. "No, that's not strictly true, because there's only one kind. Get this straight. Even if I weren't planning to turn myself in tomorrow I wouldn't toss you a nickel. The longer you put off reporting me to the cops to make me sweat, the more trouble you're in for not going to them sooner. That's accessory after the fact. We'd both end up in the slam and the odds are it'll be the same one, and that's when I'll get you."

He was scared. His jaw was slack and his eyebrows were trying to climb up into his hairline. He was young, not more than twenty-five. This was his first shakedown. He hadn't planned it, just saw his opportunity and seized it. I felt sorry for him the way I felt sorry for Godzilla when the Japs left him for dead at the bottom of the ocean.

"Sing me a ballad," I told him. "About where Reliance fits into this. About who you're working for and why. About why you've been shadowing me. And look out for the sour notes, because I'm a music critic from way back and I'll know when you're off key."

His breath was whistling in his throat. I relaxed my grip long enough to let him fill his lungs, then tightened up

77

again. Still he didn't say anything; that damn motto was too deeply ingrained. I didn't have time to debrief him, so I just held on until his face took on the proper shade of purple.

"Our client isn't a who," he gasped, when I gave him room again. "It's a what. Reliance is on permanent retainer from a coalition of major steel mills to maintain surveillance on United Steelhaulers at the executive level. Your conversation with Montana's secretary today was monitored. What you said about Bingo Jefferson's murder interested the brass. I was detailed to observe you."

"You've got a tap on Montana's telephone," I said. "That's illegal. Were you detailed to put the squeeze on me?"

The smoke from my cigarette made his eyes water. Fat tears rolled down his cheeks. He was growing younger before my eyes. "That was my idea. You won't tell them." His expression was pleading.

"Hell, they'd probably give you a raise for dedication to company policy. As long as a man like Montana heads up the union he's a threat to the big mills. Your agency's job is to get something on him that'll make him easier to deal with. If he refuses, the mills can make it public, and if it's bad enough the steelhaulers will take care of the problem for them. Reliance Investigations. 'Sneakery, Perfidy, Skullduggery.' Give me your wallet."

I released him and stepped back. He stared, looking more afraid than he had when his throat was in my grasp. He had been reared in a family whose possessions meant more than eating and breathing.

"You're right," I said disgustedly. "This entire day was part of an elaborate scheme to separate you from your pocket change. The cops were in on it and so was Montana. The corpses were papier-mâché. My name isn't even Walker. Under this clever disguise I'm actually Clifford Irving. Hand it over."

He hesitated another beat, then fingered a black morocco billfold out of the inside breast pocket of his jacket and extended it. He carried less than fifty dollars, but there

78

were enough credit cards in fold-out plastic windows to strangle a gorilla. That would be company policy as well; no cheating on expenses for a Reliance man. I lifted his photostat license, then out of curiosity unsnapped the photograph section and spent some time studying a picture of a petite-looking blonde in a light blue pleated blouse closed at the neck with a green brooch. She looked like eighteen trying to look twenty-one. Behind that was a snap of a pair of towheaded kids, boy and girl, splashing in a wading pool in a grassy backyard beside a garage with a basketball hoop mounted over the door. They might have been three and two. There were individual shots of each of them behind that, taken in a photographer's studio. I looked up at Albert Gold.

"Yours?"

He craned his neck to see what I was referring to, then nodded. I thrust the wallet back at him savagely. There are a lot of things I don't like about being single, but looking at pictures of someone else's children is the worst. Besides, it made it harder for me not to like him.

He watched, horror-struck, as I tore his license into tiny pieces. "You won't believe it," I said, dusting the bits off my palms. "Maybe you never will, but I'm doing you a favor. Go back to Lansing and tell your boss you quit. Punch him in the nose if you feel like it, but first make sure there aren't any witnesses around or you'll wind up in court. Go home. Get a job selling real estate. Shoot a few baskets. Make another kid. Otherwise the ones you have will wake up one of these mornings to an explosion and the Medical Examiner's staff will have to come around and scrape you off the ceiling of your garage. Maybe your wife will be up there with you, or one of the kids. Bombs are an equal opportunity destroyer."

"You're letting me go?"

I hadn't gotten through to him. You never do when they're that age. I lifted my glass from the nightstand and gulped. The liquor had gone flat, like my brain. "What do you want, dinner? Don't forget your coat."

He stood there a moment longer, fidgeting, then turned

and left. Back to report. I heard his wheels tearing hell out of my lawn as he backed around the Cutlass.

You never know whether it's better to let a guy like that go or to turn him over to the cops. As often as I'd seen the pictures, I never could remember if it was priest Pat O'Brien or gangster Jimmy Cagney who as a kid got collared and sent to the reform school in *Angels with Dirty Faces*, but I knew it had a lot to do with how each of them turned out. Not that I had any choice, with my description on every police radio between here and Canada.

The suitcase was a neon sign. I put it away and changed my clothes, choosing the suit that didn't wrinkle easily. The gun and holster went onto a different belt. Then I called for a taxi and left the address of the bar around the corner. The first thought the cops would have after finding my car here and me gone would be to call the cab companies. Their having to sift through all the fares coming from the busy nightstop might buy me a few hours' sleep. I grabbed my coat and hat, made sure that Gold had remembered his coat, dropped a razor and a new tube of shaving cream into the pocket, then locked up and legged it to the bar, feeling as inconspicuous as an orangutan in Hudson's lingerie department.

12

THE MOTEL ROOM HAD A WORKING RADIO, WHICH AT FIFTY
dollars a night was a real bargain. The news reports that
night spent a lot of time on tornado damage in northern
Monroe County and no time at all on Krim's murder. A
sniper had put a bullet through the windshield of a steelhauler's rig from an overpass above the John Lodge late
that afternoon. No one was hurt, and the culprit was gone
by the time the cops arrived.

The next morning, after I had shaken the moss out of
my head, they started off with the killing at The Crescent.
Dave the cop was wrong. Someone had made the connection between Jefferson and Krim, and the airwaves crackled
with speculation over whether the murders had something
to do with the impending strike. Phil Montana was un-
available for comment. The police had no suspects as yet
and were proceeding on the assumption that robbery was
the motive. They said. I turned off the radio and stumbled
into the bathroom.

I came out toweling my head, sat down next to the telephone and dialed Barry Stackpole's number at the *News*. I
heard he was back in town after negotiations to take his
crime column to network television had fallen through. A
copy boy answered and told me Stackpole had left the night
before to cover the jury-tampering trial of a former Detroit
Mafia chief in New Orleans. I thanked him, thumbed down
the plunger, and tried Getner at the *Free Press*. He was in.

"Ted, this is Amos Walker. What have the cops dug up on the killing?"

"Which one, peeper?" He didn't like me much, but he never forgot a favor and he owed me one. "We get several hundred a year. I think. The cops don't furnish body counts no more."

He hadn't heard. Well, it was early. "A guy named Krim, over at a place called The Crescent on Cass. Somebody didn't like the shape of his skull and made some modifications. You haven't got anything on it?"

"Oh, that. I got everything there is. What you want to know?"

He didn't have everything or he'd know I was a suspect. Diplomatically I said, "The radio says the cops are treating it as a robbery. How are they handling it really?"

"I'll be damned. The radio finally got something right. You called it, shamus."

I rumpled my already rumpled hair. It didn't make my thoughts any less confused. "What about suspects?"

"Zilch. Zip. Police Are Baffled. The butler was in the pantry with the downstairs maid and Cousin Roderick was at the polo matches. In other words, they don't have the proverbial pot."

"Sure they aren't holding out on you?"

"Listen, Walker." His tone grew raspy. "I've been covering cophouse six years. The commissioner doesn't change his brand of toilet paper I don't know about it. The uniforms are out pulling in the usual ex-cons and hopheads and the C.I.D. is making out its robbery statistics. If they were handling it any other way you'd read it in the afternoon edition."

"Thanks, Ted. This makes us even."

"That's what you think, gumshoe." He banged off.

I sat and thought and reached inside my shirt pocket for a smoke, then realized I'd used my last one the night before. It wouldn't have helped. Ted Getner was a bastard, but he was the best reporter I knew after Barry Stackpole. If he said the cops were approaching Krim's murder as a robbery, that's the way they were approaching it. The cop at the diner had mentioned a lieutenant. I wondered if that was Fitzroy. If it was, there was no way the janitor would sell him on a screwy angle, and in any case there was no reason he should want to, especially not after I had promised him a hundred bucks and delivered an Excedrin headache. I considered calling John Alderdyce to find out what was what, but as long as there was a bare possibility that Getner was wrong and there was a warrant out for me I wasn't about to risk a trace.

That left the question of a trap, but I wasn't worth all that time and trouble even if I had murdered Jefferson and Krim. Anyway, there's no need for that Mission Impossible stuff when standard operating procedure is so effective.

There were two ways I could play it: Lie low and let whatever was going to happen happen without my interference, or keep my appointment with Mrs. DeLancey and proceed until the long arm of the law snared me—or not, as the case may be.

There was never any choice in it, not while I still had two thousand dollars' worth of Ann Maringer's diamond ring in my pocket. A private eye with a code may be nothing more than a pebble on the beach, but at least he stands out from the grains of sand. I washed and shaved and hailed a cab for home and my own means of transportation.

THE HOUSE LOOKED INNOCENT ENOUGH. THERE WERE NO machine guns poking out of the windows, no unmarked vans parked in the neighborhood, no lineman looking nervous and uncomfortable atop the corner Edison pole. I peeped inside my car. No one was hiding in the back seat. There was no reason for anyone, not even Fitzroy or Cranmer, to plant a bomb under the hood, but I opened it and checked anyway before I got in and started the engine. I was halfway to Grosse Pointe before the back of my neck stopped tingling, and even then I made an ass of myself circling blocks twice when I was sure I was being followed. Paranoia is easier to catch and harder to shake than the common cold.

I'd calibrated each of the five buttons on my car radio

to give me a jazz station. Today four of them were playing progressive—Miles Davis and Bird Parker with music to shoot up by—and the fifth had on Sarah Vaughan. I hummed along with "Dancing in the Dark" and found myself identifying with the lyrics. I hadn't the faintest notion what I hoped to gain from this morning's visit.

A mile of private road wound among sixty-foot pine trees to the DeLancey estate, a sprawling brick ranch style on the shore of Lake St. Clair, really just a broad spot in the Detroit River separating Michigan from Canada. It was the first nice day of spring. Last night's rain had washed away the oppressive humidity. Sailboats sprinkled the lake, tiny bursts of color against the reflected blue from the sky. Birds greeted each other in the trees, and a squirrel bounced across the road in front of the car, paused, and got going again just as the front wheel was bearing down on it. They all play like that, but they don't always win. Squirrels are the private investigators of the animal kingdom.

A bright red Trans Am, parked in the circular driveway, was being waxed by a chauffeur straight out of P. G. Wodehouse—powerfully built, in puttees, jodhpurs, and a white shirt open to the navel and folded back at the cuffs. I pulled up behind the car far enough back to prevent my trail of dust from drifting over its spotless finish and got out. The chauffeur, dark-complexioned, black of hair and moustache, and handsome in a Gulf Stream kind of way, stood kneading his yellow chamois cloth and sneering at my car and, as I approached, at my suit. It hadn't borne the wrinkles nearly as well as I'd hoped.

"Nice car," I said. "They pay you to drive it?"

The sneer sharpened. No one sneers quite like a Puerto Rican. "I weesh," he replied. "The car, she belong to *Señor* Jack, the *señora*'s son. He drive, I take care. Eef not for me, the engine she seize up for no oil, the block she crack for no water. I drive the Mercedes for the *señora*." He indicated the attached garage.

"Not the same."

He rolled his eyes. "Ees like drive the jar of mayonnaise."

"How long have you been working here?" I stripped the top off a fresh pack of cigarettes and stuck one in my mouth.

"*Siete años*. Seven years."

"Then you knew the Judge."

His face shut down like a ticket booth window at a sell-out. I'd taken him for no more than thirty, but when he did that his skin broke into dozens of sharp creases. He was older than I was, though by how much I couldn't say. "I drive the Mercedes, I take care of the sport car. You have questions you go up to the door and ring the bell. The maid, she is *mi esposa*. My wife. She take you to see the *señora*, you ask her the questions. *Comprende*?"

"*Comprendo. Y saludo.*"

His features crumpled up some more. *"Por qué?"*

"It takes hard work, twenty-four hours a day, to hold on to a Spanish accent after seven years in Grosse Pointe. Or do you have a coach?"

He said something you won't find in a Spanish-English dictionary, but by then I had my back to him and pretended not to hear.

The porch was built of redwood planks ten inches wide and ran the length of the building. I pushed a doorbell button of artificial mother-of-pearl set in bronze scroll-work. Distant chimes played a familiar tune I couldn't quite remember. A lot of silence followed. I had my cigarette half smoked and was about to ring again when the door opened its full width. A pretty, brown-skinned girl in a maid's uniform said, "Yes?"

I said, "He has good taste."

A little line appeared between her rather thick brows. "I'm sorry?" It was the voice that had answered the telephone last night. Though she had an accent it wasn't nearly as obvious as the chauffeur's, nor as phony.

"*Su esposo*. He is a fine judge of feminine beauty."

She blushed, or seemed to. It had been so long since I met a girl who could that I was no longer any kind of judge.

"Gracias, Señor—?"

"Walker. I have an appointment with Mrs. DeLancey."
I handed her a card with just my name printed on it. They
still pass them around in Grosse Pointe, though not as much
as they used to. She glanced at it, asked me in, and took
my hat and coat. Her high heels clicked efficiently on the
parquet floor going away.

The entrance hall was horseshoe-shaped, closed in by
curving walls of crinkled yellow plaster made to look like
adobe. A ceiling of translucent colored glass or acrylic allowed sunlight to cast a mosaic over the floor's glossy surface. Arches opened on either side, the one to my left
affording a glimpse of rust-colored carpet, more artificial
adobe supported by what looked like real redwood columns, more redwood in the furniture, and framed Russells
and Remingtons depicting Indians and buffalo and hell-for-
leather cowboys and red-eyed steers pounding clouds of
fine yellow dust out of parched desert. They might have
been originals. The arch opposite that one led into a room
or passage paneled with knotty planks eighteen inches wide
and rough as forty acres of unplowed field. The barn they
had come from had been old at the time of Pontiac's siege.

I had finished the butt and opened the door to ditch it
when the maid returned. "Mrs. DeLancey will see you
now."

Her English was impeccable, if a little too precise. I had
a notion to advise her to slur her consonants and toss out
such lines as if all the newness had worn off them on their
way to her lips, but it would have sailed right past her.
Give her another seven years. I followed her along the
rustic passage and through another arch into the damnedest
room I had ever been in.

It was an acre across, sunken, and carpeted in mottled
orange and black. The walls were paneled in the weathered
stuff of the passage and hung with paintings commemorat-
ing more dusty scenes from the Old West. A diorama of
Custer's Last Stand fully eight feet square dominated the
space above the mantel of a fireplace large enough to play
handball in, the latter built of charred, angular stones a
little smaller than the ones Polyphemus hurled at the fleeing

86

Argonauts. A flintlock Hawken like the ones mountain men used to carry was perched horizontally below the painting, a powder horn hanging from a leather thong beside it. There was no ceiling; the roof peaked seven feet above my head, the airspace between webbed with rafters, again of redwood, from which hung a chain attached to a chandelier made from a Conestoga wheel. The rim was studded with candles that I suspected hadn't seen a flame in nearly a century.

Something was missing. I looked around and finally spotted it mounted over the arch I had just come through, a set of longhorns with a twelve-foot spread, black at the tips, and polished to a high ivory gloss. Burnt-orange curtains obscured a picture window across from me and, presumably, a view of Lake St. Clair beyond. I was tempted to stride across and draw them open just to make sure they didn't conceal a desert dotted with yucca and bleached buffalo bones. Whoever had decorated the place had not taken the term *ranch style* lightly.

"Are you properly impressed, Mr. Walker?" asked the woman standing below me in the middle of the great room, next to a man in a soft gray suit. "The frontier was my husband's first love. Perhaps his only love. Like all hobbies, I'm afraid it carried him away at times. Will you have tea?"

I said I might be persuaded. She said, "Three teas, Carmen."

The maid favored me with a polite glance that was as good as a curtsy and passed me on her way out.

"I'm Leola DeLancey. This is Daniel Clague, my attorney." Smiling the way she had in her photograph, as if she felt like blowing up at somebody but was too refined to do so in polite company, the woman held out a slender hand. I descended the three steps to take it. Her grip was strong and cool. She was my height and thin as a wire, and the simple one-piece sheath she wore with a cord knotted loosely around the waist did nothing to distract from her gauntness. If anything, it accentuated it. She had very high cheekbones and straight thick brows over gray eyes, and her chin came almost to a point. Her hair, pulled back as before and caught with combs behind her head, was silver with a bluish tint.

Clague was two inches shorter, squarely built but beginning to sag in all the standard places. His hair was brown going dirty gray. He had a broad, sad face with slack jowls and dewlaps over the corners of his downturned mouth and bags that pulled at his milky eyes to reveal scarlet crescents beneath the whites, which he sought to hide by wearing black horn rims. His hand was spotted and flabby, and after grasping it I wanted to mop my palm with my handkerchief but couldn't think of a way to do it without offending him. He didn't look happy to see me. I had a hunch he wouldn't have looked happy to see the Second Coming of Christ if he had ringside seats and a cut of the gate.

"Thank you for consenting to this interview, Mrs. DeLancey," I said.

Her eyes scoured the back of my skull. "You're welcome. Now that we've been gracious to each other, we can sit down and attend to business. Let's talk about Janet Whiting."

13

I TOOK POSSESSION OF A CHAIR UPHOLSTERED IN AN INDIAN rug design, canted backward slightly and closed in on three sides with flat wooden panels like a box. Opposite this and its mate on the other side of a Wells Fargo strongbox reincarnated as a tea table stood a couch modeled after the same design, on the edge of which perched Leola DeLancey. Clague remained standing behind it. I asked if she'd mind my smoking.

"I'd rather you wouldn't, Mr. Walker. My husband was the last person to use tobacco in this house. I don't approve of the habit."

I had one out already. I put it away. It was a shame. If ever a room was designed to be smoked in, this was it.

"Now then," she said. "What's your interest in the late Mr. DeLancey's relationship with the Whiting woman? You said something over the telephone about a murder." She saw me glance at the lawyer. "You can speak in front of Daniel. I asked him to be here."

"As a matter of fact I insisted upon it," put in Clague. His speech was slow and monotonous, like a record winding down. "It was a concession on Mrs. DeLancey's part after refusing to take my advice and cancel the interview. As her attorney I feel that any contact with this woman or her representatives would be detrimental to her interests, particularly at this time. Mrs. DeLancey's interests."

"Those interests being Mrs. DeLancey's attempt to have her husband declared legally dead," I prompted.

He looked surprised. Anyhow, his lower lip descended a quarter inch, opening a black inverted U in the bottom half of his face. It made him look like a fresh-caught bass. "Where did you learn that?"

"Don't act like you're shocked," his client commanded. "We've been at it a solid year now. It was bound to get out." Her eyes darted back to me. "I'm waiting for an answer to my question."

The maid came in with three white china cups on a silver tray, put it down on top of the strongbox, and fussed about laying out white linen napkins and silver spoons and a mirror-finish antique sugar bowl worth as much as my car. I waited for her to leave, but the lady of the house was staring at me impatiently. I tasted my tea and set the cup down in its saucer and never touched it again. Even so, that put me one up on both of the others.

"First I'd like to make it clear that I never said I was representing Miss Whiting, nor anyone else, for that matter."

Clague said, "Are you saying that you're acting on your own behalf?"

"No, I'm not saying that. I'm telling you what I didn't say." I took a deep breath and told as much of it as I thought they were entitled to hear: Of my being called by a woman who gave her name as Ann Maringer and her reasons for hiring me, of my finding the dead man in her apartment, of my interview with Phil Montana, who told me that Ann Maringer was Janet Whiting and that she had vanished last year as Judge DeLancey's heirs had begun proceedings to have the Judge declared legally dead. I was still talking when Mrs. DeLancey interrupted.

"You say that as if you think the two incidents are related."

"Are they?"

"Don't answer that, Leola."

She didn't look at the lawyer. The maid shifted her weight delicately to remind her mistress that she was still there. Mrs. DeLancey asked her to open the drapes. Lake St. Clair leaped out at me, so blue it hurt to look at it.

"If there is any connection I know nothing about it."
She switched to the offensive. "What led you to Phil Montana?"

"Didn't I say that the dead man in the apartment was Montana's personal bodyguard?" I rewound the conversation in my mind. I had said that. She shook her head.

"It's too thin. If that were what put you onto him you would have gone to see him right away, the palace guard notwithstanding. By your own admission you waited more than twelve hours. Something else happened to make you think he was involved. What was it?"

I met her level, level gaze. The cops could take lessons from the widow DeLancey. I got the box out of my pocket and opened it, holding it out. Her eyes remained on mine for an instant, then lowered to take in the jewelry. Clague leaned over her shoulder, adjusting his glasses.

"Ann Maringer—I'll call her Janet Whiting, for clarity's sake—gave me the ring as a retainer," I said. "I took it to an expert, who identified the setting as the work of a jeweler Montana uses exclusively. Montana told me he'd had the ring made for Miss Whiting as a favor to the Judge. Do you recognize it, Mrs. DeLancey?"

"No," she said dryly. "But then a man doesn't usually ask his wife for her opinion on a gift for his mistress, does he?"

"That depends on the man. Or the wife."

"Or the mistress."

"The world thrives on contrast." I closed the box and put it away. "Have you ever met Miss Whiting?"

"Careful." Clague laid a pudgy, speckled hand on her shoulder. She didn't shake it off right away. Well, they were old friends. She opened her mouth, then closed it. When it opened again:

"I almost said no. I've nothing to gain by lying. I met her twice. The first time was at the coast guard station the day Arthur's plane was reported missing over Lake Superior. I don't recall what was said; we were both in too much shock over what was happening. Of course I recognized her from her photographs. The second time was a

91

year ago in Probate Court. Daniel and I were in the judge's chambers, discussing the procedure involved in having Arthur declared dead. Jack was there as well. My son. She burst in unannounced and demanded to be heard. Babbling something about a later will naming her as Arthur's chief beneficiary. When the judge summoned the bailiff to remove her she became hysterical. She had really to be carried out bodily, screaming imprecations all the way.''

''Imprecations?''

''At the judge, me, everyone. Daniel?''

Clague nodded gravely. ''A demented young lady. A pathetic case.''

''Do you think there was anything to her claim?''

''Claptrap!'' the lawyer exclaimed.

''Excuse me?''

''Claptrap.''

''Thank you. That's what I thought you said.''

''No such will exists,'' he continued. ''I was Arthur's attorney for seventeen years. If there were such a document I would have known about it, because I would have drawn it up. Not that I wouldn't have tried to dissuade him from a course so preposterous.''

''Do attorneys usually have attorneys?''

He screwed his face into an expression someone had told him was wry. ''Of course. A surgeon doesn't remove his own appendix.''

''Not unless he's on Blue Cross,'' I said, wondering what that had to do with anything.

''If you doubt my qualifications, I refer you to the firm of Burlingame and Briggs of Toledo, Ohio. I was a corporation lawyer there for eight years before coming to work for Judge DeLancey.''

''I was just curious.'' I turned to the woman. ''Exactly what did Miss Whiting say as she was being carried out of the judge's chambers?''

''Leola,'' said Clague, ''I advise you not to answer that.''

''It's all right.'' Her face was a varnished mask. ''She accused me of arranging for Arthur's death.''

92

I had been patting my pockets in search of my notebook. I stopped. I didn't think I'd have any trouble remembering this conversation.

She smiled that strained smile that I was beginning to realize wasn't connected in any way with her true emotions. "Your next question will be was there any basis for the allegation. No. In your line of work. Mr. Walker, I imagine you encounter more than your share of bored housewives who have fallen out of love with their husbands, monied shrews who never loved them in the first place, jealous hags who would kill rather than suffer the humiliation of desertion. I belonged to none of those categories. I loved my husband very much. And strangely enough, I think he continued to love me. He found something in the Whiting woman that I wasn't able to supply, but he never stopped caring for me. I know the torment he went through when his affair became public and our marriage was held up as a travesty before the world. It was me he was concerned about, and what it might do to my peace of mind. I had every right to leave him. You'll remember that I didn't."

"I remember." The question of why she hadn't divorced him even when he had asked her to had ranked right up there with who killed Jimmy Hoffa and whatever happened to Fabian.

"It had nothing to do with his money, as the newspapers hinted. Under the circumstances my settlement would have been queenly. Come to think of it, if I had murdered him, I doubt that I would have been convicted, such was the extent of public sympathy for the 'most notoriously wronged wife since Desdemona.' The papers' words, not mine. Certainly I would have gotten off lightly. I never entertained the thought. I couldn't bear to think of life without him.

"I won't say I bore the situation with equanimity. I knew of the affair early in its development. You have no idea, Mr. Walker, of the positive *glee* with which some friends are wont to impart news of a husband's escapades to the man's wife. I made the usual threats of divorce and sepa-

93

ration, which at that point he wasn't prepared to accept. But I could see that they hurt him deeply. He was a man trapped between his lust and his duty to wife and home. So I felt sorry for him. Maybe that's the real reason I stayed, and I'm just confusing it with love. After all this time I'm no longer in a position to say which it was, love or devotion. But I never hated him and I never felt the urge to kill him."

"How did you feel about Janet Whiting?"

Daniel Clague straightened with a long, hissing intake of breath, as if he were inflating himself. "I must warn you, Mr. Walker, of the folly of defaming a person of Mrs. DeLancey's reputation in her own home, before witnesses."

"And I must warn you, Daniel, that your shirt will burst if you stuff it any tighter." A hard glint of amusement showed in his client's eyes. "Stop talking like a lawyer and let the man do his job."

"Really, Leola, I can't see why you wanted me here if you won't listen to my advice." His cheeks looked a little less sallow when he was angry.

"As you said, you insisted." She returned her attention to me. "How did I feel about Janet Whiting? I didn't. Oh, I was curious about her at first—that's natural, I suppose—but once I had found out all there was to know I became completely indifferent. She was a gray person, living a sordid little life without goals or aspirations beyond getting her hooks into a foolish old man with money. And that, young sir, is as boring an objective as you're ever likely to find."

"How did you find out all there was to know about her?"

"You of all people should be able to figure that out." She still looked amused. "I hired a detective agency."

An alarm went off at the back of my head. "Which one?"

"I don't remember the name. It was so long ago. A big firm, headquartered in Lansing. It was recommended to me."

94

"Reliance?"

"That's it. How did you guess?"

"Blind stab. I met one of their operatives last night. He said the agency had been engaged to watch Phil Montana."

"That's interesting. But it really isn't such a coincidence, is it? It's a large company. They must have hundreds of clients."

"You're probably right." I got off that. "Can you tell me what caused the breakup between Montana and your husband?"

Out of the corner of her eye she glimpsed the maid fluttering around, straightening this and that, and dismissed her. When she had vanished down the passage:

"I don't know what broke them up. Didn't Phil tell you?"

"He said it was over some bad advice Judge DeLancey had given him. I didn't press him on it. I didn't think it was important."

"Do you think it's important now?"

"I don't know. At this point I'm sweeping up everything in sight and hoping to sort it out later. Perhaps Mr. Clague knows." I looked at him, raising my eyebrows. He shook his head gravely. Everything he did he did gravely.

"Arthur never confided anything not of a legal nature to me. And I would never have asked him about it. That was the kind of relationship we had."

I nodded gravely. Now he had me doing it. "Did he leave a large estate?"

She laughed before Clague had a chance to inflate himself again. This time there wasn't a nickel's worth of amusement in it. "Except for a trust fund and this house," she said, "you could put the whole thing in an egg cup. The Internal Revenue seized everything else. It seems Arthur was not in the habit of declaring his actual earnings. It would have been worse if he hadn't suffered a major investment loss shortly before his death. As it is we're still paying off the interest and penalties, and will be long after I'm gone."

I remembered reading about it. The crash had knocked it out of the headlines in a hurry.

" 'We'?"

"My son Jack and I. Jack Billings. The only good thing to come out of a brief first marriage when I was still in high school. He's the reason I haven't had the place redecorated. He's as devoted to western Americana as Arthur was. Personally I prefer Danish modern, but we're all slaves to our children."

"There's a rough spot," I said. "If the estate was in danger of being attached, why was Janet Whiting so hot to prove there was another will leaving most of it to her?"

"I explained that to her at the time of the Probate Court incident, in an attempt to calm her down. She said it wasn't the money, it was the fact that Arthur had meant her to have it, and that a man's last wish counted for something even if there was nothing to back it up."

"Did you believe her?"

"Would you? Don't forget the trust fund and this house. To a hoofer who had spent most of her life in cheap motel rooms it might be worth the effort."

I nodded again, emptily. It seemed a year since my last cigarette. "She hasn't tried to reach you since Probate Court?"

"She said that, Walker." Acid had begun to burn through the lawyer's officiousness.

"Not exactly, counselor." My fingers itched for a gavel. "She said that she had last seen Miss Whiting a year ago. That's not the same thing."

"Objection overruled." She was smiling again, with all the warmth of an Eskimo's elbow. "As far as I know, Mr. Walker, she ceased to exist after that confrontation."

"One more question," I said.

"I should, hope so," snapped Clague.

I ignored him. "Lee Collins, the pilot who was killed with your husband and his aide. Can you tell me anything about him?"

A puzzled crease marred her smooth forehead. "Lee Collins. I'm sorry, the name means nothing to me. I'm afraid I was one of those typical society matrons who never interfere in their husbands' business. It caused me some real problems once he was no longer here to conduct them. I have Daniel to thank for bringing order out of chaos."

"I'll bet."

"What's that?" the lawyer flared.

"Nothing." I got up. "Well, I can't think of anything else. Unless you can shed some light on Bingo Jefferson's murder. Or on Krim's. I imagine you've heard about that one by now."

"I understand the police are denying that there's any connection," said Clague.

"There's no law compelling a policeman to tell the truth, Mr. Clague. Or am I trespassing on your territory?"

His rheumy eyes narrowed behind the heavy spectacles. "You're a very easy young man not to like Mr. Walker."

"I lie awake nights worrying about it." I looked down at Mrs. DeLancey. "If you still have the information Reliance gathered on Janet Whiting, I'd like to borrow it."

"I burned it after Arthur was killed. I didn't think there'd be any more use for it. I'm sorry."

"No need. You've been a great help. And thanks for the hospitality. I don't see much of it in my business."

"Nor I in mine." She raised a hand. "Good-bye. I hope you find what you're looking for."

"I wish you the same."

14

CARMEN, THE MAID, MET ME IN THE ENTRANCEWAY. I looked for my hat and coat. She didn't have them.

"Mr. Billings would like to speak with you."

"Mr. Billings?"

"Mrs. DeLancey's son." She hurried out through the arch on her left without having met my gaze once. I was beginning to think her blush was real.

The room beyond the arch was a smaller version of the one on the opposite end of the house, only there was a suspended ceiling and the western artifacts were crowded closer together. A bronze casting made from Remington's "The Scalp" stood atop a pedestal table that had been fashioned entirely of elk antlers by the hand of some rude frontier artisan long since gone to bones and dust. I knew the casting was a copy because the original was in the Smithsonian. At the moment it was being fondled by a burly party in his mid-thirties wearing a canary yellow jacket over a lavender shirt open at the neck, and white bellbottoms. As I entered he looked up, took his hands away from the statue, and smiled, displaying a natural gap between his front teeth under a reddish handlebar moustache.

"Very pleased to meet you, Mr. Walker," he said cheerfully, bounding forward to seize my hand in both of his. They were broad hands and strong despite their lack of calluses. "I'm Jack Billings. You were just talking to my mother."

His face was wide without being fat, topped by waves

of brown hair as thick and soft as butter. His eyes were gray, like his mother's but not as hard. He had an unremarkable nose, and his smile was as genuine as a congressman's expense voucher. Outfit and all, he looked like something you'd expect to find on a used car lot.

"What did you want to see me about, Mr. Billings?" I had to unscrew my hand from between his palms. He was one of those who like to hold on.

"Let's go up to my study."

The damn place was lousy with arches. We passed through another one and mounted another set of three steps. Since the house was constructed on different levels, this put us a floor above the room in which I had met Mrs. DeLancey and her lawyer. This section was paneled entirely in redwood. We stopped before a heavy, worm-eaten door that looked as if it might have been borrowed from a fashionable hotel built before the turn of the century. Billings got out a leather key case, but before unlocking the door he pushed aside a hinged section of molding, inserted a key in a hidden slot, and turned it until something clicked.

"Burglar alarm," he explained, replacing the molding. Then he manipulated the lock and opened the door, ushering me inside with a flamboyant gesture.

When I entered I saw why. Glass cases like the ones above Mike Pilaster's junk shop lined the walls from floor to ceiling, inside of which stood rows of rifles and shotguns linked together with chains like a Georgia road gang and pistols and revolvers of every make and caliber were mounted on pegs. A squat wooden desk crouched on legs carved in the shape of lion's paws between horizontal display cases sheltering more small arms on red plush with a yellowed paper tab bearing typewritten identification beside each. None of the pieces was less than ninety years old, and some sported sinister-looking notches on their grips. A portrait of Judge DeLancey, wearing riding clothes and holding buckskin gloves and a quirt, hung on the only clear section of wall behind the desk. An electric humidifier hummed in one corner.

"This was my stepfather's study." Billings waved me

into a quilted black leather chair. "I've left everything just as it was. Not out of any devotion to the old man's memory, but because I always admired his collection. Let me show you the prize." He unlocked one of the glass cases beside the desk, lifted out one of the revolvers, and brought it to me, cradling it in both hands like a bottle of rare old wine. It was a Navy Colt with an ivory grip and a seven-and-a-half-inch barrel.

I said it was nice.

"Wait," he said, and turned the butt toward me. The name "Wild Bill" was neatly engraved on the end of the brass frame.

"Not Wild Bill Elliot, the great cowboy star?"

"Hardly. It was among the items auctioned off in Deadwood to pay for Wild Bill Hickok's funeral after Jack McCall killed him in 1876. Later it came into the possession of Sheriff Pat Garrett of New Mexico, who used it to kill Billy the Kid. There's a guy out there now who thinks he's got the genuine article in his collection, but it's a fake. This is the McCoy. I've got the pedigree, a letter signed by Garrett himself."

"Impressive. Is that why you asked me up here?"

The eager light faded from his eyes. "No." Reverently he replaced the gun in the case and locked it. Then he sat on the edge of the desk. "I wanted to set you straight on some things my mother told you."

"What'd you do, bug the room?"

He flushed. "No, and I resent the implication. Carmen told me."

"I see. May I smoke?"

"Please do. I don't myself, but I've missed the smell of tobacco around the place since Arthur died. He was partial to pipes."

"I'm not." I fired up a weed. "You'd better watch that stuff with the maid. Her husband has a bad temper."

He glared. "Do you want to hear this or not?"

"I'm all ears, Mr. Billings."

He nodded once, stiffly. He'd put me in my place. "First of all, Mother lied when she said she didn't know why Phil

Montana broke up with Arthur.'' He smiled sheepishly. "Carmen didn't stop overhearing things when she left the room.''

I watched him through the smoke. He continued.

"In a way, Montana lied too. While it's true that the rift opened over some poor advice he got from my stepfather, that advice had nothing to do with his duties as Montana's legal counsel.

"I was passing the study one day when I overheard Arthur on the telephone. The door was open. He was speaking in that tone people use when they're trying to calm someone down—slow, soothing, as if they're speaking to a child. He addressed the caller as Phil. He knew only one person by that name.

"I gathered that Montana was angry about a stock tip he had gotten from Arthur. It seemed that on my stepfather's advice, Montana had directed United Steelhaulers' accountant to invest union funds in a company called Griffin Carbide. I did some reading about it later. Griffin was a small firm, barely making ends meet, but the rumor was that it was going to merge with an eastern conglomerate. When that happened the stock would go through the ceiling. Anyway, the rumor turned out to be false, Griffin went under, and Montana had to face the union rank and file with the news that their retirement fund no longer existed. It says something for his popularity that he was re-elected by a landslide after he finished his sentence for assault and was finally allowed to participate in union politics again. But it hurt the union, and because of that he dismissed Arthur as his attorney and never spoke to him again.''

"Would that be the major investment loss your mother mentioned?'' He nodded. "Are you sure she knew?''

"She knew. Don't be taken in by her uninterested wife pose; that's just something she developed as a shield against the IRS. Which is probably why she played dumb, in the interests of consistency.''

I smoked and thought. "You said there were 'some things' you wanted to set me straight on. Plural. What else?''

"Second." He got up, walked around the desk, and unlocked a drawer. He had a key fetish. After rummaging around a little he drew out a sheaf of dog-eared pages bound in manila covers and came over and dropped it into my lap. I opened it to the first page. The title was typewritten, centered in caps.

CONFIDENTIAL: JANET WHITING
RELIANCE INVESTIGATIONS

I looked up. He had perched himself on the edge of the desk again. "Mrs. DeLancey said she burned the report."

"She asked me to do it. I didn't. I thought it might come in handy."

"Fond of the women, aren't you, Mr. Billings?"

I thought that might offend him, but he merely shrugged. "I've made my share of conquests. I'd seen Miss Whiting a number of times without actually having met her. She was a beautiful woman. It was her eyes that set her apart. Maybe you noticed them."

"I noticed them." I looked around for a place to tap my cigarette ash. He plucked a heavy brass ashtray off the desk and reached it over. I balanced it on the arm of my chair and used it. The silhouette of a bison was embossed in the bottom, what else? "I guess I'm hopelessly cynical," I said. "Whenever someone does something generous for me I can't help wondering what he wants in return."

"I'm concerned about Miss Whiting," he said sadly. "I always have been. The press made her out as some kind of tramp because of her past and because she was going around with a rich man old enough to be her father. After I read that I knew different." He indicated the report. "Read it, Mr. Walker. You'll find a warm, caring person inside. She deserved better than she got, and I want to do everything I can to help her get it."

I flipped through the report absently. Then I closed it. "What do you stand to gain from the will?"

He looked suspicious. "That sounds mighty like an accusation, pardner. I was vacationing in Hawaii the week my stepfather disappeared. I still have the hotel stubs if you want to see them."

"Not necessary."

"Besides, my share of the trust fund is nothing compared to what I got from him when he was alive. He was guilty about his situation, which made him a soft touch where Mother and I were concerned. His death cost me plenty. You think I'm callous, don't you?"

"What I think wouldn't pay the toll at the Windsor Tunnel, Mr. Billings." I took a last drag on the cigarette and mashed it out on the bison's head.

"We weren't very close, Arthur and I," he said. "I was an adult by the time Mother married him, so he missed being a father figure. I made an effort to interest myself in his investment business, but he seemed to prefer casting me in the role of the no-account playboy stepson. So I took the part. I'm not a strong person, Mr. Walker. I tempt easily. I was sorry when he died, but if I shed any tears, it was for the end of the easy life."

"You said you'd like to help Miss Whiting get what she deserves. Did you mean the so-called later will?"

His expression was smug behind the handlebar. "I don't believe there is a will. But if there is, she's entitled to benefit from it, wouldn't you say?"

"Yeah, maybe you two could split the trust fund and cut out the old lady."

He got up and stood looking down at me, with his fists clenched at his sides. "Stand up." His voice was choked.

"I was out of line, Mr. Billings. I apologize."

"I said stand up!"

I met his gaze. "I said I was sorry. You don't want to take it any further."

"Damn you, no one insults me in my own house! Stand up or I'll give it to you where you sit!"

I started to rise. He hurled a respectable haymaker at my jaw that might have been trouble had it connected. I caught it in one hand and stepped to one side, and twisted his arm back and braced my other forearm against the stiffened elbow. He cursed through the gap in his teeth. I said, "I don't want to break your arm, Mr. Billings. I opened my big mouth and you probably have a right to bust me one, but I'm too well trained to let you do it. Please accept my apology.''

"I accept." It was a croak.

I released the arm. He stumbled forward, caught his balance after a few steps, and leaned against a glass case, working the abused limb. He took out a handkerchief and mopped his face. Beneath his breath: "Well, Jack, you made a horse's ass of yourself again."

"Not a horse's ass. Just a poor judge."

"You're very kind. I think."

"Thanks for your help, Mr. Billings." I picked up the report from the floor where it had fallen and rolled it up, just to have something to do with my hands. "By the way, did you happen to know Lee Collins, Judge DeLancey's pilot on that last flight?"

He shook his head, smiling helplessly. He was almost back to normal. "As I said, he never took me into his confidence. I never met most of the people he did business with."

"How about Krim and Bingo Jefferson? Did you know them or why they may have been killed?"

He smiled the same smile. "I'm sorry."

I thanked him again and made for the door. Then I turned back. "Does the Judge's collection include any thirty-two caliber pistols or revolvers?"

"Several. They weren't as common out West as the forty-four, but they were far from rare."

"Would you know if any of them is missing?"

"Of course. But I can see them all from where I'm standing. Wait a minute." He crossed to DeLancey's portrait and swung it out from the wall, revealing a round metal safe recessed behind the woodwork. "He acquired an old Forehand and Wadsworth thirty-two a few months before his death. A derringer. It was said to have belonged to Doc Holliday, but there was no verification. He was in the habit of storing handguns in this safe until they could be authenticated." He gave the dial a final twist and pulled open the door. He put his hands inside, there was a pause, and then I saw his shoulders tense.

"This can't be," he whispered.

15

I JOINED HIM AS HE WITHDREW A GRAY METAL STRONGBOX from the safe's interior. His leather key case still dangled from the open lid. The box was empty. I glanced inside the safe. The tiny light that went on when the door was opened glowed yellow over loose papers, a ledger with brass corners, a triple-deckered checkbook, nothing more.

"When was the last time you saw the gun?" I demanded.

Billings continued to stare at the box as if by sheer force of will he could make the derringer return. "I don't know." His voice was dreamy with mild shock. "I've had no reason to check as long as the box was in its place. I don't think I've seen it since before Arthur—"

"Was anything else kept in it besides the gun? Cash? Jewelry?"

"Just the Forehand and Wadsworth. Now I remember. The last time I saw it was the day Arthur sold me the collection."

"He sold it to you when?"

"Just before I left for Hawaii on that vacation I told you about. Come to think of it, that was the last time I saw Arthur."

"Didn't you wonder why a fanatic collector would up and sell you the lot just like that?"

"Not at all." He lowered the lid and put the box back in the safe, returned the key case to his pocket and swung the door shut. A hidden spring whirled the dial to some innocuous digit. Then he replaced the painting. "He knew that if the Internal Revenue seized it, the collection would be sold at auction, the pieces scattered God knows where. He'd spent years building it up and he couldn't stand the thought of it. He made the deal on the condition that no part of it could ever be resold. I signed a paper in agreement."

"Where'd you get the money?"

He smiled ruefully. "I borrowed it. When you're in debt as often as I am, your credit rating is A-1. It's one of the benefits of being broke in this great land of ours."

"Could the Judge have taken the derringer with him on that last fishing trip?"

"Possibly. I can't think why, since it would technically be stealing. If he felt he needed protection, he owned several modern pistols, all registered and legal and infinitely more reliable than any of these relics."

I could think of a very good reason, but didn't mention it. "Does anyone else have the combination to that safe?"

"As far as I know, I'm the only one. Of course, I have no way of knowing if Arthur gave it to someone else. That's highly unlikely, however. He was a cautious man. Anyway, I alone hold the key to the burglar alarm, which I had installed myself."

"There's nothing in that. There are a hundred and ten ways to get around the most sophisticated alarm system in the world. They're the first things a second-story man learns. Or it might have been lifted while you were in Hawaii, before the system was installed."

"They'd still need the keys to the door and to the strong-box."

"DeLancey had them."

Deep in thought, he said nothing.

"What about your mother?"

"I'd sooner suspect the mayor. The only things Mother hates worse than tobacco are guns. She's terrified of them, to the point of refusing to enter this room."

"That leaves the servants. And Clague."

He laughed shortly. "Clague wouldn't have the guts.

107

He's been sweet on Mother since the day she married Arthur, but hasn't even had the nerve to tell her in the five years my stepfather's been dead. As for the servants—'' He shrugged. "Not Carmen, though. Never Carmen." He was silent for a moment. Then his cheeks flushed. "Damn! If that does turn out to have been Doc Holliday's weapon and the thief doesn't know it, it might be used in some nickel-and-dime stickup and end up on the bottom of the river. Think of the loss to posterity.''

"You think of it. I don't have time." I went back to the door. "When the police question Mrs. DeLancey, you'd better tell them about the gun. If it turns out to be the one that killed Bingo Jefferson and they find it, they'll be all over you. That's friendly advice in return for your cooperation. You can do what you like with it.''

He nodded. Then he looked worried. "Do you think that's true about Julio?''

"Julio?''

"The chauffeur. Carmen's husband. You said I'd better watch it because of his bad temper.''

"Yeah. He's in pretty good shape and he moves like a boxer. And Puerto Rico's national bird is the switchblade.''

"Thanks. I'll remember that.''

"Por nada." I waved the battleworn report he had given me and went to collect my hat and coat.

THE HOOD WAS UP ON MY CUTLASS AND THE DARK CHAUFfeur was leaning over the engine. I crept up behind him softly and thrust a stiffened forefinger against his spine. He tensed.

"Qué pasa, Julio?" I spoke through my teeth.

He straightened slowly and turned to face me. His dark Latin eyes fell to my empty hand. He smiled sneeringly, white teeth gleaming against his brown skin.

"I was admiring your engine, *señor*. Ees a beautiful machine. *Pero no está original.* Also illegal.''

"I didn't like the one it came with," I said. "I had the pollution equipment removed from this one because I could have eaten my lunch in the time between when I stepped on the gas and the carburetor got the message." I put a cigarette in my mouth and offered him the pack. "You spent a lot of time with Judge DeLancey, didn't you, Julio?"

He accepted one, smoothed it between his even brown fingers, and stashed it in his shirt pocket. His expression was guarded. "Maybe. *Cuánto dinero, señor?*"

As I replaced the pack I tapped my wallet part way out of my inside breast pocket and thumbed the corner of a sawbuck into the open. My coat shielded it from the house. He glanced at it and nodded almost imperceptibly. I said, "Let's take a look at the spare."

He slammed down the hood and we walked to the other end of the car. I unlocked the trunk lid and threw it up, blocking the view from the windows. I got out the ten spot. He eyed it hungrily.

"*Sí,*" he said. "*El juez,* he was a busy man. I drive him everywhere." He reached for the bill. I held it back.

"To the airport?"

"*Sí,* many times."

"You saw his pilot? A tall man, large hooked nose? Called himself Lee Collins?"

His eyes narrowed. "I theenk you forget how leetle the ten dollars buys today, *señor.*"

"I theenk not." I struck a match as if to light my cigarette, but set fire to the bill instead. Black smoke curled up from the burning edge. He made a grab for it. I pulled it back out of his reach.

"I see the pilot," he blurted, watching the bill anxiously. "Many times. I speak to heem some of the times. *Por favor, señor!*"

I touched the flame to the cigarette, then blew it out. One corner was gone. "What did you talk about?"

"Nothing of importance. Some of the times we drink the coffee in the lounge while *el juez* talked on the telephone. We speak of the weather, our pay, the man we work for. *Es verdad!*"

109

I had started to put another corner to the burning end of my cigarette. I stopped. He lowered his eyes.

"Hees name, eet ees not Collins. He was dark like *español*, but he was not Spanish. He had a funny accent."

I left that opening alone. "Singsong? Like an Arab?"

"*Sí*, like *arabe*. The people who are buying America."

"Did you ever catch his real name?"

He shook his head. I moved the bill closer to the Winston's business end. "Eet was funny name," he said. "I cannot remember."

"Was it Krim?"

He was ecstatic. "*Sí*, Kreem. I ask heem once and he tell me. Ali Kreem. He said everyone who heard eet accuse heem of the high gasoline, so he change."

I extended the bill. "*Gracias*, Julio."

He snatched it from between my fingers and stuffed it into the slash pocket of his jodhpurs. "Do me a favor and go straight to hell."

He stalked past and resumed waxing the already glittering Trans Am. I let him. You can't get good help these days, even when you pay them for something you had to begin with.

I'D SKIPPED BREAKFAST THAT MORNING, SO I GRABBED AN early lunch at a counter on my way to the office. The hamburger was still sitting in my stomach like a lump of lead when I went through the unlocked outer door. No one was waiting for me, and the air had that stale smell that told me no one had been. Which was a relief, because I was still expecting the cops. I left the door standing open to gather circulation from the hallway, unlocked and entered my private office, and threw open the window. Sunlight flashed off the windshields of automobiles exceeding the speed limit in the street below. I laid the report Jack Billings had given me on the desk and went back and got the mail and shed my hat and coat and opened and read the stuff on my way back to the desk.

There were no coded messages for me to decipher, no requests to trace the missing duchess, no urgent entreaties from the police to help solve the mystery of the tower room, the man with the limp, and the one-eyed Albanian dwarf. What there were were a final notice from Detroit Edison and a friendly warning from my alma mater that I was about to receive a telephone call soliciting a donation. I parked the bill with the others under the blotter and flipped the cheery form letter into the waste basket. They'd squeezed all the blood out of me they were going to get.

I turned on the ceiling light and sat down to read the report on Janet Whiting. It was written in detectivese, full of addresses and times and subjects entering and exiting buildings. The dick who had filed it used slashes and semicolons like a hypochondriac uses aspirin, but you don't get much chance to refine your writing skill sitting in an automobile with one eye on a newspaper and the other on the door of the building across the street. After a few paragraphs I found myself counting the pages that remained.

The background stuff was better, though hardly illuminating. She was born thirty-eight years ago in Huron, a village thirty miles west of Detroit, to George and Elizabeth Stephens Whiting. Her father was fifty-two at the time of her birth, her mother forty-six. She spent what the bread advertisements would call her formative years doing the things small-town girls usually did twenty-odd years ago and seldom do anymore, until the company her father worked for moved its headquarters to Detroit and the family was forced to follow. At that point things went sour.

Three weeks after the move, her mother collapsed while crossing Livernois and died of heart failure before the ambulance arrived. Never prosperous, the two survivors found rates hostile on the west side and wound up in a two-room apartment on Hastings, a street that no longer exists, on the theory that when a neighborhood goes bad, building an expressway through it will eliminate the problem.

At the age of fifteen, less than a year after leaving Huron, Janet was arrested and fined for prostitution. More arrests followed, some for soliciting, others for nude or topless dancing in neighborhoods where zoning laws prohibited such goings-on. Meanwhile her father died. She

111

was twenty-seven and dividing her time between go-go dancing in several downtown joints and selling her favors in an apartment on Erskine when she happened to meet Judge Arthur DeLancey while the latter was waiting at a taxi stand and she was getting out with her companion for the evening. The companion was sloppy drunk and she was delivering him home. She didn't have carfare and when she and the hack went through her escort's pockets it developed that neither did he. The hack was all set to holler cop when DeLancey slipped him enough to cover the tab and to help carry her customer up to his apartment. After that he offered to share the taxi with her. She accepted, and the two sped off in front of a sidewalk full of witnesses. End Part One.

I flipped back through it absently, wondering why someone with enough on the ball to sit on the federal bench could let himself be seen in the company of a prostitute. I wondered about other things as well, such as why page three of the background section was lighter in color than the others.

Like the others, its corners were bent and thumb-blurred, but while the rest had yellowed slightly, this one remained as white as the day it had left the cellophane. I studied it more closely, comparing the typescript. The characters on this page were a shade blacker than those on the preceding and succeeding sheets. I flipped the page back and forth, back and forth. The characters differed in style as well. Why not? They had been typed on different machines.

Carefully, I closed the cover and undid the metal clamp that bound the sheets through holes punched in the margins. Then I removed page three and laid it next to the others. While the holes in these pages showed the natural wear incurred by something round impaled by something flat and carried around for a while, the holes on the sheet in question were sharp and new.

For no reason other than to gain time to think, I put the whole thing back together and set it aside and sat staring across at this month's calendar shot of a tall blonde caught bathing under a waterfall. For once I wasn't looking at her.

112

I was thinking about Jack Billings and what reasons he might have for replacing a page of the report. Then I stopped thinking and dialed the DeLancey house. The maid answered.

"Hello, Carmen, this is Amos Walker. I was there earlier. Is Mr. Billings in?"

She answered without hesitation. "I am sorry, Mr. Walker, but Mr. Billings left a few minutes ago for the airport. He is going on vacation."

"Going on vacation where?" We both answered in unison: "Hawaii."

I thanked her and hung up. My hand was still on the receiver when the door opened and Lieutenant Fitzroy came in, followed closely by Sergeant Cranmer. They looked unhappy.

16

"WELL," I GREETED, CASUALLY SCOOPING THE RELIANCE report into the top drawer and pushing it shut, "if it isn't Cheech and Chong. Which one gets the straight lines today?"

"What a dump." Cranmer, bareheaded, his color grayer and looking more unhealthy than ever against the bright plaid of his sports jacket, dragged runny eyes over the bubbled wallpaper, the weary customer's chair, the flies trapped in the ceiling fixture.

I said, "Bette Davis. Now do a hard one."

Fitzroy, everybody's favorite uncle, smiled sadly. He was wearing a green suit today, with a polka-dot tie and his narrow-brimmed hat. There would be poems about that hat on the men's room walls at police headquarters. "You're funny," he said. "Like a leak in an oxygen tent you're funny."

Policemen's patter. It doesn't change from year to year, and though it darkens with age it never shows wear, like government green or the linoleum in a third-floor back apartment. It was old stuff when some dick used it in Plato's time, but every cop who employs it acts as if he wrote it that morning. He expects applause and when he doesn't get it he tends to get mean. A mean cop is not a pretty sight any time of the day. In the morning it's worse. I smiled engagingly.

"What brings you to poverty row?"

"So witty after such a busy day and morning." Fitzroy

lowered himself into the customer's chair and placed his hat on the edge of the desk. His hair looked indecently yellow in the morning glare streaking in through the window. I got up, drew the blinds, and resumed my seat. His bright little eyes followed every movement. "I thought you might want to rest after spending the last twenty-four hours hotfooting it ahead of the hounds."

"Come on, Fitz," I said. "We're old friends now. You don't have to be coy with me. You're upset about something."

He rose and with one arm swept everything off my desk. The lamp, the blotter, the pen set that hadn't worked in two years, the unpaid bills, the telephone, his hat—everything went crashing to the floor. The bulb in the lamp blew with a report like a pistol shot. Even Cranmer jumped.

"Jesus," said the sergeant.

"I'm Fitz to my friends and other cops." His partner was leaning over the desk with his fingers curled under the edge. He wasn't shouting—his smile hadn't even faltered—but in the silence that slammed down on top of the sudden din he might as well have bellowed. "To you I'm Lieutenant Fitzroy."

I got up and gathered the stuff from the floor and put it back where it belonged. I even retrieved his hat and set it where he had set it. Before replacing the receiver on the telephone I listened to see if it was still working. It was. If General Motors built their cars with what Ma Bell puts into her instruments there wouldn't be a body shop left in business. I resumed my seat.

"That'll be a buck for the lightbulb," I said quietly. "Edison doesn't give them away anymore."

Cranmer, over his shock now, sneered. "Hell, you're not so tough."

I ignored him, watching Fitzroy. "Just because I don't dump my clients' money into plastic plants and a blonde in the front office with calluses on her back doesn't mean the place is condemned. Pay up or get out. I'll take the sight of your fat butt waddling through that door in trade."

The sergeant stepped forward, drawing his head down

between hunched shoulders. "Just say 'sic 'em,' Lieutenant. We can tell the skipper he fell downstairs."

His partner was still watching me, still smiling. It could mean anything. In his position he could reach me easily with one of his small, hard fists or dump the desk over on top of me. I braced myself to meet his move, whichever it turned out to be. Outside the seasons went on changing.

He said, "Give him a buck."

Cranmer's jaw met the floor with a clunk. He turned to gape at his superior.

"Go on, toss him a one-spot. I guess that's his price today." Fitzroy's eyes never left mine. They were kind eyes, humorous eyes. Like Janet Whiting, he had been put together by partners who never spoke to each other.

"Not mine," I said. "Edison's."

Painfully, like a professional virgin saying yes, the sergeant hauled a tattered leather billfold from his hip pocket, peeled it open, and thumbed through some bills inside. There were a couple of crisp singles that hadn't been in circulation long, but he went past them and settled on a fuzzy one that someone had used to mop out a grease pit. He flung it down on the desk, from where Washington's dirty face leered up at me like a syphilitic degenerate. I pushed the eraser end of a fresh pencil under the crease, lifted it, and draped it over the telephone.

"I'll spray it later."

He growled and started around the desk. I rose to meet him.

I said, "Let's do it. Two moves, maybe three, and you'll be a detour in the street. I've had three years of martial arts training courtesy of Uncle Sam and he's been waiting eight years to get his money's worth."

He blinked stupidly. Then he smirked and continued coming. I readied myself. In another moment I was going to rupture him. How long his partner would let me live after I had was immaterial. It was going to be worth it.

"Down, Prince," Fitzroy said. "Anyone can see you eat nails and wash them down with battery acid."

116

"You heard him asking for it, Lieutenant. That jujitsu crap don't scare me."

"Nothing scares you, does it, Roy? Except maybe me."

There had been no threat in his tone, just straightforward logic. Yet the sergeant's gray face went ashen, and he resumed his former position on the other side of the desk. I made a mental note to ask John Alderdyce about those two the next time I saw him.

"You too, op," said the lieutenant. "Looking up at you puts a crick in my neck."

I decided not to tell him where he gave me a pain. "I'll sit if you will."

We sat. Our relationship got more juvenile every time we met. Pretty soon we'd be scraping lines in the dirt with our shoes and daring each other to step across them. I lit a cigarette and flipped the match into the ashtray with a picture of Grand Traverse Bay in its base and waited for him to begin. I didn't wait long.

"We picked up Franklin Detwiler at Metro. I guess you know who he is."

I said I'd heard the name. He was plucking at something on the knee of his trousers and looking at it. I leaned forward to see past the edge of the desk. There was nothing on the knee of his trousers.

"He told us he'd been paid by Phil Montana to let Bingo Jefferson fill in for him at The Crescent, and that after Jefferson was iced Montana paid him again to blow. We also talked to his girlfriend, Coral Anthony. She told us you'd been to her apartment and talked to her. We went over and talked to Phil Montana. He told us you'd been to his office and talked to him. We got the squeal on a shooting at The Crescent. Krim wasn't in any shape to talk to anyone ever again, but the janitor told us you'd been there and talked to *him*. Just now we called Leola DeLancey and she told us you'd been out to her place and talked to her. I figured maybe we could save the trip to Grosse Pointe by coming here and talking to you. If you don't have laryngitis from all that talking." He looked up at me through his pale eyelashes. He was as coy as an avalanche.

117

"You'd be missing a lot," I said. "It's a nice day and the view of the lake is a honey."

"Does that mean you aren't going to tell us what you found out?"

"I couldn't tell you anything that you don't already know, or couldn't learn at the library. You've spoken with Montana. He gave you what he gave me or you wouldn't have known about DeLancey. Mrs. DeLancey said her husband was having tax trouble at the time of his death. She said his mistress was screwing up their attempt to have the old man declared legally dead by claiming the existence of a later will naming her as chief beneficiary. Her son, Jack Billings, told me that Montana and his stepfather broke up over a bad stock tip on DeLancey's part. Something called Griffin Carbide that dropped out of sight faster than the Susan B. Anthony dollar. I have no idea where that fits in or even if it does, but it's yours for nothing. That's the kaboodle."

"You're forgetting something. A ring."

"I didn't forget it. I left it out because I didn't think you came here for a crash course in deductive reasoning. The ring's what led me to Phil Montana, who set me straight on Ann Maringer's real identity. You've got that."

He was looking at me squarely now, no false modesty, no picking at nonexistent imperfections in his clothing. His smile broadened. He and Leola DeLancey would like each other. "I'm kind of peculiar," he said. "I don't like the *Reader's Digest* version of anything. I like unabridged stuff. Let's see the sparkler."

I produced the box and opened it for his edification. Cranmer moved in for a closer look. When he reached for it I slapped the back of his big hairy-knuckled hand. He withdrew it, snarling.

"We'll just take that," said Fitzroy.

"Not without a warrant." I tapped the lid back on and returned the box to my pocket.

"I don't see how you've stayed in the game this long, the way you cooperate." It was the first time he'd seemed

118

human since he cleared my desk. I disliked him a little less this way. Nevertheless I got mad.

"When is your kind of cop going to learn that cooperation doesn't come free? Don't look do damned snide; I'm talking about courtesy, not graft. I could maybe forgive what happened yesterday morning at headquarters. You had a murder on your hands and I was the most likely suspect. But you can't barge into a man's place of work and do a bad impression of Barton MacLane from an old Bogart flick and expect him to fall all over himself making your job easy. You want something, do it by the book."

He listened without interrupting. Then: "I suppose the same goes for whatever that was you ditched in your desk drawer when we walked in."

"The same," I acknowledged. "You can take your suspicions over to the Frank Murphy Hall of Justice and convince the judge it wasn't this month's *Field and Stream* and come back with a warrant."

"We can pull you in on suspicion of murder. Krim's murder this time."

"Warrant."

"We can put you in custody as a material witness."

"Warrant."

"We can arrest you for obstruction of justice, which in this state can tie you up in the courts longer than a homicide rap." I started to open my mouth. "Don't say it!" Color bled into his cheeks. "There's one thing I don't need a warrant for, and that's yanking your ticket to practice. I've got friends on the State Police."

"I'll get a hearing, and the board will want to know why you parked Krim's murder around the corner. Why did you, by the way?"

He stood and looked down at me. I hoped that didn't hurt his neck. "I could have put out an APB on you, had you in the cage by this morning," he said. "I didn't, because I wanted whoever knocked down the Arab and made it look like robbery to think we'd bought the scenario. I've been a cop for sixteen years and I know a big case when I'm involved in one, and this one's so big I can't see around

119

it. Phil Montana's mixed up in it somewhere and so is Mrs. DeLancey, and your client's smack in the middle of it. And you know where that puts you.''

"Right at the top of your S-list," I responded.

"Not just mine. Your friend Montana makes out like he's the Lone Ranger and the Scarlet Pimpernel rolled into one, but you know and I know that while he was in the slam the boys with Italian names and monogrammed violin cases got their hooks into United Steelhaulers but good. They don't like publicity. Joe Columbo liked publicity. He liked big crowds and applause and microphones and TV cameras and his picture on the front page. He got lead in the head and a speaking acquaintance with a turnip.'' He picked up his hat from the desk. "Be smart, Walker. Don't tell the big mean cops nothing on account of they spilled your dominoes. I'll come visit you someday in the produce section of the supermarket.''

"Nice to see they're zipping up your dialogue," I commented. "I suppose the next we can expect is a funny neighbor. Maybe you'll get picked up for another thirteen weeks.''

"I'm laughing. You better hope the button men they send after you have my sense of humor.'' He pulled on his hat and went out through the open door. He walked with a peculiar skip that blew a hole in his huff. Cranmer hung back.

"Next time maybe he won't be there to interrupt us," he said quietly. I told him to go eat a Buick.

After he had gone I finished my cigarette. Then I got up and went through the outer office and stuck my head out and looked up and down the hall. Cops set a lot of store by eavesdropping. When I was sure they had taken the stairs I closed and locked the outer door from the inside and went back into my private office and sat down behind the desk and opened the deep drawer.

I wasn't after the bottle. I forget how exactly, but sometime within the past couple of years I had acquired a directory of Michigan newspapers. It almost never came in handy, but I can never bring myself to throw anything away. I lifted the three-inch-thick volume onto the desk, waited for the dust to settle, and began paging through it swiftly.

The *Herald* was Huron's only newspaper, a weekly. I pulled the telephone close and dialed the number listed there.

17

THERE WAS NO ANSWER, SO I SMOKED ANOTHER CIGA-rette and tried again. Still nothing. I frowned at the instrument. I couldn't afford to wait. By now Fitzroy was talking to a judge, and I didn't want to be there when he and Cranmer got back with a warrant. I left the Reliance report behind for seed and went out to get my tank filled.

Afterward I got change from the attendant and pulled my car around to the side of the station and called the *Herald* a third time from the pay telephone. Same story. I looked at my watch. It was past one o'clock, but you never know when anyone's at lunch these days. Then I remembered Albert Gold's business card. I wasn't sure I had transferred it to this suit along with everything else from the pockets of the one I'd been wearing the night before, but I found it finally and gave his home number in Lansing a try. The whole world was out today. I had no reason to expect him to cooperate anyway, even if he had access to his agency's report on Janet Whiting, which I doubted. I used the same dimes on another stab at the newspaper.

"Huron *Herald*."

It had purred only once before the brisk feminine voice came on the line. I blanked out for a moment.

"Huron *Herald*," repeated the voice, a trifle irritated this time.

"Is this the Huron *Herald*?" Well, it was something.

"No, it's the local office of the CIA. We answer the phone this way so the Communists won't know we're here.

You aren't a Communist, are you?'' The woman's tone rang with irony. It wasn't a young voice, but it refused to be dated. There was a twang somewhere under the polished shell, maybe Kansas.

"Not at the moment." I introduced myself. "I'm a private investigator engaged to verify information included in an employment application to my client's firm. The applicant, a woman named Janet Whiting, claims to hail from Huron. I wonder if your newspaper might have anything on her in its files."

"May I ask the name of the firm?" I heard the racheting sound of a fresh sheet being rolled into a typewriter.

"Michaeljohn International." They had hired me once to look into a suspected employee theft.

Typewriter keys plock-plocked in the distance. "When does she say she lived here?"

I gave her the dates. She tapped them out.

"Her address in Huron?"

"Four–four–two–six Agar Lane. Sounds like it's in the country."

"It is. Or it was, until the subdivisions started gobbling up all the available farmland." She was typing as she spoke. Only reporters and doctors can divide their concentration like that.

She asked me a few more questions on the same order and plucked out the answers as I gave them. The operator came on the line to tell me my three minutes were up. I was about to deposit some more coins when the woman said, "Save your money, Mr. Walker. This will take a while to check. Would you care to come out this afternoon? I should have the information by the time you get here."

"I wasn't planning to make the trip. Can't I call you back?"

"That would be your loss. It's too nice a day to waste in the city." She said "city" as if the word tasted unpleasant.

"You've persuaded me. How do I find the place?"

"You're a detective. Detect."

"Who should I ask for when I get there?"

123

"Anyone you ask will be me. It's a one-woman office. Just for the record, though, the name's Maggie."

I grinned. "Thanks, Maggie." The operator cut me off in the middle of it.

Half an hour on the Edsel Ford took me into another world, of rolling hills and tilled farms and jaded cows that raised their heads to watch the hissing traffic like patient old men on bus stop benches watching pigeons strut past on the sidewalk. The Huron exit channeled me onto a winding paved road past a tiny factory, a lot of houses less than ten years old, between two sprawling brick schools with rows of yellow buses parked in a lot, and finally into the village proper. At this point the road merged with another blacktop at the V of a tiny park to form a main street as broad as Woodward Avenue but a hell of a lot less congested. False-fronted buildings as old as the state charter lined the street for two blocks, after which it narrowed to pass beneath a stone viaduct and on to more villages like this one and yet not like it at all. I had the crazy notion that if I kept driving I would continue to encounter similar communities, factories, houses, and schools until I eventually came back to Detroit, towering over them all like the manor of a feudal estate that encompassed the globe.

The *Herald* occupied half the ground floor street frontage of a three-story building between the bank and a meat market and was identified by faded lettering on a plate glass window seven feet high and four feet wide. I pulled into an empty space in front of it and cranked a coin into a meter so old it still took pennies. A partition separated the office from the TV repair shop next door. This week's issue was in the window and the glass in the door had an amateurish cartoon taped to it of a woman with a camera over her shoulder hurrying out a door over the promise BE RIGHT BACK! I tried the door's brass handle. It was locked.

Twenty minutes and two cigarettes later, a wiry, sixtyish woman in a rust-colored pantsuit came clicking down the sidewalk with an early-model Polaroid slung over one shoulder from an elastic strap. She had pure white hair combed into brittle waves and wore glasses with jeweled frames attached to a black cord that went behind her neck. Her tiny feet were encased in brown leather half-boots with square, two-inch heels, which as she approached made her only a foot shorter than I. I looked from her to the cartoon in the window and back to her. It was a fair likeness.

"You're Mr. Walker." The way she said it brooked no denial. She had bright hazel eyes that darted from behind her glasses, and her handshake was firm. "I hope you haven't been waiting long."

"Depends on what you call long," I said. "The Count of Monte Cristo wouldn't have considered it any kind of wait."

She produced a key from her purse under the Polaroid and inserted it in the ancient lock. "I had to take a picture of a group of cheerleaders. Those entertainers you see on television balancing spinning plates on flimsy rods never tried to get six high-school–age girls to smile for a camera all at once." She opened the door and ushered me inside.

The room was narrow, about eight feet by twelve, painted bile-yellow, and made even more cramped by two scarred desks on opposite ends and a black iron safe that didn't look much older than a Ming vase, although it would be considerably less fragile. A stack of copies of the current edition stood on the near desk, next to a child's red metal bank labeled DEPOSIT 15¢ PER ISSUE. There was a big square heat register in the floor inside the entrance. Beyond that, an unevenly faded red carpet was just something to cover the broken tiles. The ceiling was eleven feet high. An electric typewriter, the only modern thing in the room aside from the telephone on the far desk, stood on a rickety stand in that corner.

She charged past me, parked her camera and purse beside the newspapers, and went through a door in the end wall marked EMPLOYEES ONLY. A moment later she came out carrying a black-bound book fully eighteen inches wide and thirty inches long and thumped it down atop the far desk, after first sliding the telephone out of the way. As she was opening it to the page she had marked with a sheet

125

of newsprint, I peeped through the open door at a dusty old platen press.

"Do you print the paper here?"

"Not in twenty years." She found her place on the page and adjusted the book so that it wouldn't slide off the desk. It contained bound copies of the *Herald*. "We're printing in Jackson now, which is one more step away from the paper's original ideals about remaining local. Next month we're remodeling the office. The TV shop next door is moving and the partition will come down and we're going to put up snazzy paneling made to look like wallpaper and drop the ceiling and change the carpet and scrap the Linotype and presses in back. We'll get rid of the furniture that's been here for half a century and replace it with vinyl-upholstered chairs and desks that look like folding card tables. The place will be modern and functional and as antiseptic as a dentist's thumb. I've already given notice."

"You're not the owner?"

She laughed shortly. "This is just a hobby for the owner, who runs a bigger, slicker paper upstate. I'm just the typical town gossip who started with a gloppy column about senior citizens and suddenly found myself the staff writer. Staff writer, that's what they call me. Takes up less space than editor, bookkeeper, receptionist, photographer, ad manager, and janitor. Pull up a chair." She sat down behind the desk. Although she had the antique swivel chair screwed up as high as it would go, her shoulders barely came above the edge of the big book.

The only other chair in the office was a wooden straight-back behind the other desk. No one had sat in it for a while. I dusted off the seat with my handkerchief and carried it to her desk and sat down.

"Do you mind if I smoke?" I got out the pack.

"Go ahead. What do I care if you shorten your life?" She pushed over a cheap tin ashtray and watched while I went through the ritual. When I had one burning: "First, let's talk about who you really are and who you represent."

I gave her my best dumb look. I could have saved myself the trouble.

"I looked up Michaeljohn International." Her angular chin and the straight line of her mouth formed a perfect square. "They make the bolts that are used to fasten wooden packing crates going overseas. I wondered why they'd bother to hire an investigator to verify the details in a prospective employee's application, not being the kind of firm that handles a lot of classified material. Also, no P.I. working for a big company like that is going to make a long distance call from a booth. He'll make it from his own phone and charge his client as if he'd paid for it on the spot. Then he'll turn around and take it off his income tax."

"You have no reverence for the profession," I suggested.

She looked at me levelly. "Eighteen years ago I divorced my husband. I'd hired a private investigator to follow him and gather evidence on the affair he was having with a fellow employee. He got it and sold it to my husband. No, I have no reverence for the profession."

"It's not fair to judge an entire group on the behavior of a single individual."

"Maybe not. But I believe in the odds. If the only P.I. I hired in my entire life turned out to be crooked, the chances are that the majority of them can't be trusted. You haven't answered my question, Mr. Walker. Who are you and who do you represent really?"

I leaned forward and tapped my cigarette ash into the tray. Then I remembered that I was still wearing my hat and took it off and hung it on my crossed knee. I'd left my coat back in the city. "What difference does it make? If you don't trust me you aren't going to give me the information I'm after anyway."

She smiled and reached out to pat my hand. I could have fallen off my chair. "I said I didn't believe you. I didn't say I wouldn't help you. Your client is none of my business. Like I said, I'm the town gossip."

I grinned. "Maggie, you're priceless." Her answering smile shone beatifically with the aid of store-bought teeth. "I can give you this much. I've been hired to find Janet

127

Whiting. She may be in danger, and the danger may have something to do with her life here in Huron. But it may be tied into a bigger story, and for what it's worth I can promise the *Herald* exclusive rights to print it in return for whatever help you can give me."

"You're sweet, but what works with the big city papers holds no water out here. We're a weekly. Unless the dope gets in just before noon Wednesday we get scooped by every daily in the state. But you can give me five dollars."

"Noon Wednesday," I said, getting out my wallet. "I'll remember that." I laid a fin down on the yellowed newsprint in the book. A bony hand scooped it up and deposited it in the flap pocket of her jacket. She saw me watching and winked.

"The boss needn't know about it." Then her eyes dropped to the closely printed page and she ran a long finger down the third column until she reached the bottom. "Hold onto your Victorian values," she cautioned. "This is juicy stuff."

18

I GOT UP AND PUT MY HAT DOWN ON THE CHAIR AND walked around to her side of the desk to read over her shoulder. The issue was dated twenty-four years ago. The item she was pointing to at the bottom of the column was less than half an inch long.

> Mr. and Mrs. George Whiting and daughter Janet are moving to Detroit this week, where their new address is not known.

"I see what you mean," I said, straightening. "My heart's all a-flutter."

She said, "Stop being sarcastic and sit back down."

I responded to the authority in her voice, going back to my chair and returning my hat to my knee. I wondered if she had ever taught school. "This better be worth five dollars and the trip out here. What's written there I knew before I left the city."

"I don't guarantee that what you get will be worth your time and expenses," she retorted. "Do you, in your line of work? Anyway, it's a good story. Too bad a family paper like the *Herald* couldn't print it." She swung the big book shut and removed her glasses, letting them dangle at the ends of the cord around her neck. Her eyes looked sharper without them, like unsheathed daggers.

"My reaction was the same as yours when I saw that personal," she began. "We still get them, though not as much as we used to, and use them as filler. 'Minnie Grubb spent last weekend visiting her son and daughter-in-law in Benton Harbor.' That sort of thing. But that 'their address is not known' intrigued me. Why say that? On a small-town paper, when you can't find something out you just don't mention it; there's no sense in advertising your inadequacy. There were two other 'moving' items in that week's issue, and neither of them included an address nor apologized for the omission. Seen in that light, the disclaimer in the Whiting piece took on a special significance, as if it was some kind of snide innuendo on the writer's part. So I started asking around.

"I've lived here only fifteen years, and I couldn't find anyone who had been around at that time who remembered the Whitings. Apparently they kept to themselves, because there was nothing about them in any of the other papers I read. As a last resort I drove out to the Methodist Home and spoke to Agnes Gooding. She held down this desk for seventeen years, until she suffered a stroke eight years ago that left her deaf in one ear and confined to a wheelchair. She remembered Janet Whiting very well indeed."

She paused. I smoked and waited. When it became evident that I wasn't going to press her, she continued.

"Until her husband died and she moved into the village, Agnes lived next door to the Whitings. Janet was a shy girl, rather awkward because she was growing up too fast physically. She loved movies and romantic stories. In those days the old theater was still operating and she went down there every Saturday night. Every week the garbage can in front of her parents' house was jammed full with trashy magazines—love stories and like that. She probably wasn't a good student, because with all that dreaming she wouldn't have had much time for homework. I can't verify that; fourteen years ago the old school building was gutted by fire and all the records were destroyed. Fortunately, this was stored in a corner where the flames didn't reach."

She extracted a thin volume from the deep drawer of the desk and opened it atop the bound newspapers. For some time she flipped through slick pages covered with pictures of boys in football uniforms and girls in cheerleaders' sweaters until she came to a two-page spread of inch-square portraits and swiveled the book toward me, placing a finger on a picture in the third row. A plain-looking girl with straight dark hair cut in bangs across her forehead looked back at me with eyes as big as half dollars. She wasn't smiling.

You see them in every high school yearbook, the one member of the class who has nothing to smile about. It was just a picture, one millisecond out of a lifetime, but it said more to me than anything else had thus far in the investigation. I said, "She doesn't look happy."

"There's no reason she should," said Maggie. "That was taken during her freshman year, the year she left town. Agnes said she tried out once for the cheerleading squad but didn't make it, probably because she was too gangling to perform the routines. Not long afterward her parents enrolled her in a dancing academy in Ann Arbor, ostensibly to teach her grace. Agnes doesn't know what the results were."

"I do," I said. "She could dance rings around Travolta."

"You couldn't prove it by me. I'm still coming to the juicy part. You know that she left town with her parents at the age of fourteen. What you don't know is why."

"My information is that the firm her father worked for moved to Detroit."

"That much is true. But that wouldn't have made them move. George Whiting retired the year before."

I dragged all the good out of my cigarette and killed the butt in the ashtray. "That I didn't know."

"I said so. Janet wasn't a particularly pretty girl. She was too tall and hadn't learned yet how to handle herself. But she had beautiful eyes, according to Agnes. Big, blue, and innocent. Details like that are very attractive to some men."

"I'm beginning to get what you mean."

"There's a house out on Pinedale Road," she went on, ignoring the comment. "It belonged to one of our leading

131

citizens—meaning richest—who died about three months ago. It's a secluded place surrounded by woods and overlooking a private lake. The owner used to rent it out during the summer to folks from the city.

"Twenty-four years ago, a man who gave his name as Peter Martin was living there. Fortyish, Agnes said, dark and rather handsome in a brutish sort of way. He was seen in town only once, when he stepped into the hardware store to buy fishing tackle. Janet Whiting happened to be in the store at the same time, running an errand. They were seen talking, and after Martin had made his purchase they left together. The clerk gathered that he had asked her for directions to someplace, and assumed that they had gone outside so that she could gesture.

"An hour later, George Whiting called the store looking for his daughter. When the clerk told him what had happened, he called the police. They went out to the house on Pinedale, and sure enough, there was Janet. Martin told the officers he had merely invited her over to sample some of the trout he had caught that morning, in return for the help she had given him in finding the place he was looking for. She backed him up, and since she didn't seem to be harmed they took no further action, just brought her home. A week later Martin went back to Detroit. That might have been the end of it, except that the Whitings left town after another few months. Agnes said that Janet had begun to gain weight by that time."

"Does she think she was pregnant?"

Maggie smiled wickedly. "The odds are in favor of it. But I'm still coming to the good part.

"The clerk wasn't the only witness to what happened in the hardware store. There was a customer, a retired truck driver, who had seen Martin a couple of times in Detroit, though they had never actually been introduced. Only he knew him by a different name."

I waited. Her smile was diabolic, her eyes sharp as glass shards.

"Phil Montana," she finished.

* * *

THE TELEPHONE BELL MADE ME JUMP. SHE SPEARED THE receiver and barked the name of the newspaper into the mouthpiece. Someone wanted to place a classified ad. She put on her glasses, jotted down the information in shorthand on a yellow scratch pad, got the caller's name and address, read it back, said, "Thank you," and hung up. Her eyes returned to me.

"Caught you off guard, didn't I?"

"It wasn't the name I expected," I admitted. "Is this truck driver still around?"

She nodded. "In the cemetery west of town. He's been dead ten years at least."

"The house on Pinedale. Who owns it now?"

"Some firm in Detroit; I don't remember the name. It's been closed for some time. Would you like me to look it up?"

I shook my head. "Do you think they'd mind if I drove out and took a look at the place?"

"They don't have to know about it. The less anyone in that city hears from us, the better. But you'll never find it by yourself. I'd better go with you."

"What'll it cost me?"

"Not a damn cent." She stood. "School's letting out right now. There are a couple of little girls that run over here every afternoon and beg me to take their picture for the paper. I'm too soft to refuse and film's too expensive to waste. I'd rather just be out when they get here." She went over to collect her purse.

"You're soft," I said, getting up and putting on my hat. "Like a destroyer escort."

She grinned.

We drove under the viaduct and along a scenic blacktop that wound past rows of subdivisions, stop-and-go party stores with gasoline pumps in front, an occasional lake, and a lot of real estate offices in what had been private homes. The sun was warm on the pavement, and here and there pretty girls of about seventeen were walking home from school in shorts with their books in one hand and their shoes in the other. Seeing them made me ache, not

133

from sexual frustration, but from nostalgia. My passenger rode with her eyes trained straight ahead.

"What have you got against Detroit?" I asked her.

"Nothing, as long as it stays put and leaves us alone. At the present moment, more than half of Huron's population works in the city and commutes back and forth. Nothing wrong with that either, except that the population of the village itself hasn't changed in twenty years. They come swarming out here and buy up all the farmland and cut it up into acre and half-acre lots and put up NO TRESPASSING signs like they're land barons. When I first came here there were sixteen houses along this road. Now there are six hundred. They raise their brat kids the way they were raised. As a result, we average more incidents of breaking and entering and vandalism than any neighborhood of comparable size in Detroit. And it doesn't stop there.

"Not long ago some social worker got the idea that juvenile delinquency withers and dies when surrounded by trees and grass. So they invoked public domain, booted the farmers and homeowners off the property they inherited from their grandfathers, and started building parks. All right, so the few must make sacrifices for the welfare of the majority. That's democracy. Only there are five thousand acres of parks within a twenty-mile radius of Huron and they're planning to build more. And they wonder why our grandchildren will be eating earthworms for nutrition."

"I get you."

"I'm not finished yet," she said.

"I was afraid of that."

"The city's in financial trouble. So is my brother-in-law, and for the same reason—because he can't handle money. He asked me for a loan, but what did he ever do for me? I said no. Now we aren't speaking. Fine. I never liked him anyway. But it doesn't work that way with the city. The mayor goes to his buddy the governor and says, 'Look, we need sixty million dollars or I won't be able to keep up the payments on my new limo.' The governor says, 'Sure thing; didn't you contribute to my campaign fund last election?' and kicks up taxes all over the state. When we complain he reminds us that if Detroit falls, so does Michigan. That bothers me, that does. I can just see them throwing a barricade across the state line with a sign: GONE OUT OF BUSINESS.''

"Nice speech," I said. "Except the mayor's a Democrat and the governor's GOP. They don't contribute to each other's campaigns."

"Not so you'd notice. Turn here."

A dirt road angled off to the left through steepening hills cloaked in tall trees. As we started the climb: "I bet two other people had this same conversation twenty years ago."

"Could be," she agreed. "Only it's worse since Watergate. The American people are so inured to scandal that they've given up hope on anything better."

She was silent for the rest of the trip. There were few houses in this area. Those we saw were perched atop hills and all but invisible behind shrouds of evergreen and budding maples. At length she pointed at a rutted driveway winding up through thick growth, its mouth flanked by gray concrete pillars with vines growing out of the cracks and blocked by a weathered wooden gate secured with a chain and padlock.

"We'll leave the car here," she directed. "Go up on foot."

I pulled the Cutlass as far as it would go onto the weeded apron and we got out. There was just space enough between one of the pillars and the tangled brush for one person to squeeze through. I let her go first. From there we hiked for a solid mile along the twisting path, which inclined with each turn. The earth was still moist and slippery from last night's rain. After a hundred yards I began to sweat. I loosened my tie and peeled off my jacket and threw it over my shoulder. My shirt clung to my back. Maggie, who had left her purse in the car, chugged along as steadily as if she were crossing Huron's main street. She wasn't even breathing hard. I decided it was all those years of good clean country air, and found myself hating her.

The house was an A-frame, rare in its day but now as

common in woodsy settings as gum wrappers on a sidewalk. From a high peak, the shingled roof canted all the way to the ground on either side of the glassed-in front. The glass was tinted so that we couldn't see inside.

I walked around the building while I waited for my breath to catch up with me. Behind it the hill rose for another forty feet before it rounded off, its crest jagged with pine and cedar. Maggie was standing where I had left her when I completed the circuit.

"How long has the place been empty?" I asked.

She shrugged. "The former owner stopped renting it not long before he died. Too much trouble with the tenants. No one's lived there for several months."

"Is there a caretaker?"

"Not that I know of."

"Then how do you explain these?" I pointed at the ground at my feet. She came over to look. A set of footprints showed clearly in the mud between the stone foundation and the overgrown lawn.

"A prowler," she suggested. "Or maybe there is a caretaker."

"If it was a caretaker, he'd have a key to the padlock on the gate. He'd drive up rather than suffer that hike. No one's driven up that road since the rain or there'd be tire tracks. I think we'd better—"

Inside something crashed.

19

Birds sang in the stillness that followed the sudden noise. It meant nothing to them. Up high, wind moaned in the pines, an eerie, half-human wail. We listened, but nothing significant developed.

"On the other hand, it might have been a squirrel," said Maggie. "They cause a lot of damage in these empty cabins."

"We'll know soon." From my wallet I drew my photostat license and tested the lamination between thumb and forefinger for stiffness. Then I tried inserting it between the doorlatch and the jamb. It didn't work. It never does, for me.

"What are you doing?"

I hadn't heard Maggie moving in closer. When I came down from the roof I said, "Nothing, apparently. We'll have to smash the lock."

"What do you mean, 'we,' paleface?"

I glanced at her. She looked about as nervous as a pothole in the road. "If you'd rather not be part of this, you can wait for me back at the car."

"Aren't you afraid of being eaten by a bear? That's the first thing you city folks think of when you're out in the country all alone."

"Lady, I grew up in this country, not fifteen miles from where we're standing. The nearest bear is on a billboard asking people to prevent forest fires. I won't start kicking in the door until you're out of earshot."

"Kick it in. I'm sixty-three years old and I've never seen the inside of a jail. I might as well experience everything I can while I'm still able to enjoy it."

"You'd be disappointed."

It was an old lock of the turn-and-snap variety, not a dead bolt. I shattered it in two kicks. The door flew inward and bounced back to hit me in the shoulder, not very hard. Wishing I hadn't left my Luger in the glove compartment, I motioned Maggie behind me and palmed the door open slowly, keeping to one side. No bullets ricocheted off the jamb. I stepped over the threshold.

The ground floor was all open space, with no walls to separate the porcelain-tiled kitchen from the green-carpeted living area, where a low couch and a couple of scoop chairs were arranged so that people sitting in them could look out over the wooded slope beyond the glass, at the bottom of which the road we had taken played a twisting game of peekaboo with the scenery. A corner of the private lake Maggie had mentioned was visible to one side, looking like the edge of a blank coin set in green velvet. At the other end of the room were a bar with two swivel stools uphol-stered in red leather, a small, copper-colored refrigerator, a matching two-burner stove, and a microwave oven of the same hue. The second story was really a loft, divided into two open bedrooms with a railing in front and connected to the main floor by a spiraling metal staircase, down which a man was crawling.

He made his way slowly and painfully, grasping the edge of a step and dragging his body a few inches forward and downward, then reaching out to grasp another. His face was a smear of wax in which his mouth gaped black and round. His blond hair, dark with perspiration, was plas-tered to his face like seaweed to a rock. He was gasping hoarsely, mechanically, without hope. He didn't know he was gasping. He didn't know we were there watching him. He didn't see us. All he saw was the next step down.

The debris of a lamp sprinkled the tiles to the left of the stairs where it had shattered after being dislodged from the second-floor railing. Probably he had staggered against it while making for the stairs, fallen, and found himself too weak to climb back to his feet. Behind him, the steps glistened dark and wet.

Maggie didn't scream. She couldn't have if she had wanted to, paralyzed as she was. The color of her face, or rather the lack of it, matched the man's. As I approached the stairs on jointless legs I caught a glimpse of my own reflection in a mirror on the side wall. I didn't look any more robust than they did.

He had rounded the last curve and was eight steps from the floor when he lost his grip. For a throbbing moment he hung there, one dusty palm outstretched, groping for the next step, and then the other hand, the one he was using to brace himself, let go. His chest struck the metal with a loud *woof*, and he slid clattering to the bottom, one arm still extended as if he were a runner caught off base and diving to beat the tag. He reached the tiles and skidded to a halt at my feet.

Maggie screamed then, a hoarse, masculine wail that saved me the trouble.

I waited until the body stopped hiccoughing before I squatted to feel the throat for a pulse. As often as I'd seen it in Nam, I could never shake the suspicion that they were trying to get up when they did that. This one wasn't.

Death, and the nearness of it, has a way of changing a person's features. I wouldn't have recognized him at all had it not been for his checked coat. Crazily enough, my first conscious thought was that now I knew why Albert Gold hadn't answered his telephone earlier. He had been here, dying.

Telephone. I looked around and spotted one on a stand between the chairs in the living area. I pointed at it. "Find out if that works," I directed Maggie. My voice didn't sound like anyone I knew. "Call the police."

"We don't have a police force anymore," She spoke shallowly. "There's a sheriff's substation in the village park."

"Whatever. Call them."

"What about an ambulance?"

"We don't need an ambulance."

That took a moment to register. Then she made her way to the telephone as if she had to move each foot by a separate effort of will. I couldn't blame her. This was my third corpse in a little more than thirty-six hours, and I wasn't any more in command of the situation than she was. While she was lifting the receiver I clenched my teeth, grasped the body by both shoulders, and turned it over. It was like handling a sack full of loose iron weights.

His shirt was slick with blood. I unbuttoned it, using my handkerchief, and pulled it away from the wound. It made a nasty sucking sound. The wound, half an inch above his belt, was small and blue and looked pretty insignificant to have killed a full-grown man. It could have been made by a .32. It could have been made by a .25 or by a .38; you can't tell where something soft like flesh is concerned. Whatever it was, it had been more than enough for the purpose.

"Dead."

I started to agree, but then I saw Maggie with the receiver in her hand and realized she was referring to the instrument. I folded the checked coat over the gore and rose.

"Can you drive?"

"I was handling a Hudson Hornet when you were just a gleam in your father's eye, sonny."

I smiled faintly. She was bouncing back. Women like her always did. I held out the keys to the Cutlass. "Take mine to the nearest working telephone and call the substation. I'm going to take a look around."

"Do you think the murderer is still nearby?" She came forward and grasped the keys.

"I doubt it. Where he was shot you bleed a long time before you die. The only reason he got up was he must have heard us outside. Maybe he wanted help, or maybe he thought it was the killer coming back to finish the job. Before that he was probably semi-conscious."

Her eyes flicked to the dead man. "Did you know him?"

"I met him once. I didn't like him."

"Maybe you'd better tell me the whole story."

I shook my head. "When the police get here you're better off ignorant. As a matter of fact, you're best off not being here at all. When you call them, say you saw someone walking up the road to this house and got suspicious. Don't identify yourself."

"They'd recognize my voice. I only drop into the station twice a week. They'll ask me how I got out here, with my car in plain sight back in town. What'll I tell them, I jogged six miles? Besides, they'd take one look at you standing over that body and ventilate you. The substation commander used to be a Detroit police officer."

"Which detail?"

"STRESS."

"Swell."

She said, "Listen, when they broke up the unit its members had to go somewhere. This one came here. Anyway, you promised me an exclusive."

I studied her clinically. "Town gossip, my uncle's saddle shoes. What papers did you apprentice on before you came out here?"

"Not one, but it doesn't take long to pick up the jargon. This isn't Dogpatch."

"If I say you can stay, will you go?"

She smiled weakly. "Believe it or not, I understood that. Yes."

"You got it."

When she had gone I went through Gold's pockets. Change, keys, the same wallet containing the same pictures. The girl looked prettier than last time, the kids cuter and more innocent. They didn't know they were half orphans. I smeared everything carefully and put it back. Cops are unpleasant enough without the knowledge that someone's been tampering with their precious evidence.

I looked down at the body and wanted a cigarette but didn't light one because I know what store cops set by leftover butts as clues. Scientific detection had reached the sticks about the same time as television.

Walker Investigations, my Yellow Pages display read.

141

Specializing in missing persons. What I was good at finding was stiffs. It was getting so I couldn't walk through a door without tripping over one.

Leaving philosophical conclusions to the people with brains, I circled the body and mounted the stairs, avoiding the sticky patches. The bedrooms had enough room for the beds, night stands supporting lamps with flowered china bases, and identical three-drawer dressers. The beds had the look of having been made for some time. The drawers were empty, lined with newspapers dated last year. I lifted the paper in each and looked underneath. Nothing. There were no personal articles in either room. Ditto the bathroom, a closet-sized cell behind the staircase with a sink, a commode, and a tub just large enough to wash one limb at a time.

There was dust on the furniture, not a lot of it, but enough for a house that hadn't been lived in for some time. I tried all the switches. No electricity. In short, there was nothing in the house that I hadn't expected to find, with one exception. Which left me farther behind than I had been coming in.

20

THE COMMAND OFFICER'S NAME WAS HARDACRE, AND HE looked more like a small-town cop than any other man I had ever met. He had a lot of face the color and texture of raw hamburger and scanty brown hair and Popeye forearms swelling from the rolled sleeves of his desert tan uniform shirt. He had nine years on the Detroit Police Department. The only reason I know that is he kept reminding me.

He took one look at me after coming in the door, glanced at the corpse, and detoured into the living room, where he took possession of the couch and motioned me over. He was accompanied by a pair of deputies, one tall and outdoorsy with dark hair and a seamed, windburned face; the other young, slim, redheaded. Both were wearing stiff brown felt hats with broad brims and tin sheriff's stars on the front, and the younger one was carrying a third. He approached his superior with it while his partner went over to examine the body.

"Your hat, Sergeant," he said, holding it out. "There might be pictures, and you know how the sheriff feels about deputies being in full uniform at all times."

"The sheriff can roll his hat into a tube and shove it in up to his elbow. Nine years I was a Detroit cop and I never wore one. Who's taking pictures? You see any cameras around Maggie's neck? Hello, Maggie."

The newspaperwoman, who had made it back ten minutes before, returned the greeting. She called him Fred.

"Somebody move this body?"

I turned to look at the dark deputy, who was staring at me from a squatting position beside the still form. His hands, encased in disposable surgical gloves, dangled loosely between his knees.

I said, "I did. I was trying to revive him." You tell a lot of lies in my business.

"Coroner's gonna drop a brick. He favors playing them as they fell."

"I got a hat all ready for the coroner to roll, too."

Hardacre produced a white handkerchief from his hip pocket and mopped his red raw neck. It wasn't that hot, but he was sweating. Without looking at me, he put his hand out palm up and wiggled his fingers. "The license."

I gave it to him. Lately it had been in and out more often than a family cat. He read it, every word, moving his lips, and returned it. When he wasn't paying attention I wiped it off on my pants leg and put it away.

He said, "Detroit, huh? They ever get around to swamping out that king-size toilet?"

"Some," I replied. "Mostly they just squirted some deodorizer around the bowl."

He didn't appear to have heard. "I don't go much for P.I.'s. The ones I used to do business with were mostly cops that got bounced for going on the take."

"What they bounce you for?"

I was trying to gauge his limits, but he wasn't having any of it. He used the handkerchief behind his left ear and looked at it as if he thought the red might come off. Then he spread it out on his knee to dry. He winched his eyes up to meet mine for the first time since he had come in.

"For a guy in your position you got a lively mouth."

"What exactly is my position, Sergeant?"

"Right now you're a suspect. I haven't heard your story yet. Maybe when I have we'll reduce that to witness. Providing I like it."

I gave him the story, or as much of it as I thought he needed. I couldn't tell if he liked it. I couldn't even tell if he was listening. The deputies were, particularly the young one still holding the sergeant's hat. He watched me wide-eyed, the way young law officers everywhere watch a case developing, as if they're half astonished to find themselves part of it and half fearful that someone will notice them and ask them to leave the room while the grownups talk. The dark one squatted scowling at his gloved hands still hanging unused. I wondered why he hadn't just left them bare.

When I had finished, Hardacre killed some time contemplating his drying handkerchief. Then: "That the way you saw it, Maggie?"

She moved her shoulders. "More or less. I can't say about all the details. I'm not as observant as Mr. Walker. As for everything he says went on before he came here, I'm no witness."

He nodded meaninglessly, his head bobbing like a car with bad shocks at a stop light. Then a smile tugged at the corners of his mouth, or maybe it was an attack of gas. He was still eyeing the handkerchief. "Attributing, as usual. You're one hell of a journalist, Maggie. And anyone who's more observant than you could see through six inches of lead. Any idea what this Gold was doing here?"

It took me a second to realize he was speaking to me. "I'm guessing," I said. "He may have seen his agency's file on Janet Whiting—the original, not the bowdlerized version Jack Billings gave me—and decided to check it out, as I did. I don't know why. Maybe he smelled money in it. He tried to blackmail me when he thought I was mixed up in Krim's killing."

"You said you broke the lock. How'd he get in?"

"Maybe he found the door open when he got here. Maybe the killer had a key and was ready for him. Or maybe one or the other was a better burglar than I'll ever be."

He nodded again, as absently as before. "Well, we'll sort that out later. In the meantime it looks like you got some court time coming. For breaking and entering and trespassing."

"I doubt it. About the B-and-E, I mean. I heard a noise and thought someone might be hurt and that I could help.

145

I was right about the being hurt. And trespassing stopped being a felony when they closed the frontier.''

"No kidding? They closed it? When?'' He tried to sneer, but that involved too many facial muscles and he gave up. "The point is, Walker, we got a modern department out here. Telephones and everything. I can check out your story and have you in the county lockup by nightfall. You have to admit it's pretty suspicious, you being first on the scene of three murders.''

"Suspicious, but not suspect. I'm clear with Detroit P.D. on the other two, reasonably so. As for this one, we'll let the coroner decide when he took the bullet that killed him. I've been busy today. Bet you I can prove I was thirty miles away when it was fired.''

He was watching me steadily now. His eyes were dish-water-colored. "You're smart, city fellow. Too smart and not smart enough.''

"You must sleep with a notepad taped to your stomach so you can jot down gems like that when you think of them,'' I suggested.

The dark man chuckled. I didn't look at him. Finally Hardacre rapped, "Dennis, radio Station One and have them call old man Kitchner's widow and find out who he sold this place to. Then have them get in touch with whoever it is and find out if they want to press charges against Walker for B-and-E and trespassing.''

The redheaded deputy started to leave, retraced his steps, and laid the sergeant's hat on the glass coffee table between the scoop chairs, then went out to fulfill his orders. I heard him opening a door on one of the two scout cars parked out front and wondered for the first time how they had gotten past the locked gate. Bolt cutters, probably.

"Nine years I was a Detroit cop,'' the command officer informed me. "In that time I met every kind of peeper there is: divorce peepers, missing persons peepers, security peepers, business peepers, railroad peepers, lawyers' peepers, plain old peeper peepers. I never invited one of them to dinner. You want to know why?''

"Because we pick our teeth with our thumbnails?''

146

"Because I don't like them. They all have that cheesy feel, like a paper towel in a men's toilet. Pluck one and another one just like it comes down to take its place. And not one of them worth using to wipe—"

"At the risk of destroying a delicate point," Maggie broke in acidly, "I've got a paper to put out and tomorrow's deadline day. Who's going to drive me back to town?"

Hardacre scrubbed his face again with the already sodden handkerchief. I was beginning to realize why his complexion was so rough and red. "You shouldn't mind sticking a little longer," he told her. "You're sitting on the biggest story your paper's seen in months. One murder's news out here. In Detroit they list them in columns like shipping reports."

That last was for my benefit. People who live in the country always think people who live in the city stay there by choice and ought to be ashamed. I let it flutter.

"I wonder what Gold did with his car?"

"What?" The sergeant threw me a hard glance.

"His car. You know, that thing that goes *vroom* when you push the slanty pedal and rolls away. It isn't parked at the bottom of the hill and he didn't drive it up here."

"What makes you think he had a car?" The dark deputy looked stern. "Unless you went through this pockets and found a set of keys."

"I didn't," I lied. "But I know he owned a car, or at least had access to one, and he didn't walk all this way." I described the vehicle I had seen parked in my driveway the night I met Albert Gold. Was it only last night? The deputy shook his head.

"Don't sound familiar. But Huron's a fairly busy place, full of folks driving through on their way somewhere else. An ordinary heap like that would be missable."

I turned to the newspaperwoman. "Is there another way up here?"

"None," she said. "There used to be an old logging trail somewhere near here, but that's all grown over by now."

Dennis returned, looking younger than he had going out. Hardacre questioned him with his eyebrows.

"Some company owns the place now," explained the deputy. "No one's answering the phone, though."

"What's the name?" the sergeant asked.

He got out a pocket pad with a hinged cover and flipped through a dozen or so scribbled pages. "Here it is. Griffith Carbide."

THE POP AND FLARE OF MY MATCH MADE THE YOUNG DEPuty jump. Everyone watched me as I set fire to the cigarette in the corner of my mouth. I hoped the tremor in my fingers wasn't noticeable. Slowly, reflectively, I blew out the flame and crushed the match into the tiles at my feet. A car was pulling into the driveway.

A gray-haired man with a white beard and circles under his eyes like glass marks on a bar came in carrying a black bag and made his way over to the corpse without acknowledging the presence of any of the room's other occupants. As he lowered himself stiffly to one pinstriped knee, the dark deputy got up and gave him room. Not once had the latter made use of his surgical gloves.

"When'd he get shot, Doc?" asked the sergeant.

"How the hell should I know? And don't call me Doc. This isn't a Looney Tune." His sharp, thin voice lashed out like a serpent's tongue. He felt Gold's neck for a pulse, then opened his shirt and examined the wound. His fingers were lean and wrinkled and nearly too fast to follow.

"Two hours," he said. "An hour this way or that. That's all you'll get out of me until after the autopsy. Of course the body's been moved."

"I know."

The doctor glared up at the dark deputy. "Oh, you do, do you? How many lectures have you attended on postmortem lividity? What do you know of splotching of the body's dependent parts not in contact with the surface upon which the corpse rests after death due to the settling of blood?"

148

The deputy looked embarrassed. "I just know that dead people don't usually land on their backs."

This time the old man's eyes snaked over to where Hardacre was sitting. "I'll bet you told him that," he said, and returned his attention to the corpse. "Dead people land wherever they want to land, young man. Fifteen years ago I examined a house painter who had fallen from a roof and skewered himself head first on a steel fence post. We had to unscrew him like a cap from a bottle. I'll make you a deal: I won't investigate any crimes if you promise not to engage in forensic pathology. And take off those silly-ass gloves! Harmful bacilli don't show up for at least twelve hours after death unless the body's been exposed to extreme heat."

All the time he was speaking, the doctor's hands were darting this way and that, lifting a limp arm and releasing it, bending dead elbows, poking and prodding, buttoning and unbuttoning. The younger deputy was beginning to look a little pale watching him.

"Two hours," Hardacre reflected. "Where were you at noon, Walker?"

"In my office, talking to Fitzroy and Cranmer of Detroit Homicide."

"We'll check it out. Meanwhile we've got you on the other two charges."

"Don't forget me, Fred," Maggie reminded him. "If you take him in, you've got to take me as an accomplice."

"That won't be necessary, and you know it. You were just doing your job."

"So was Mr. Walker."

"That ain't the same thing." His grammar was faltering. He was getting irritable.

"It is, and *you* know it," she pressed. "You just want to make a quick arrest and you want me out on the street so I can write it up in the *Herald*. You're transparent, Fred. It's no wonder they canned you in Detroit."

He glowered at her. The hand holding the handkerchief lay forgotten in his lap. "We got a good relationship, Maggie. Don't blow it."

"What will you do, refuse to show me your fender-bender reports? You know how the sheriff feels about good publicity. You're too close to retirement. What are you going to do if the story I write costs you those stripes and you have to live on a deputy's pension? You and the sheriff never did get along. This could be just the excuse he's been looking for to shake you out of his hair."

The room was silent but for the sounds the doctor made fussing over the body. The dark deputy was watching him like an intern. Dennis wasn't sure where to look. Maggie, smiling tightly, stared at the sergeant, who had gone back to staring at his handkerchief.

"Don't leave town," he told me finally.

I produced one of my cards and placed it on his knee. "You can't make me stay here without a warrant and you know it," I said. "But just to show you my heart's in the right place, call me there. My answering service will take a message if I'm not in." I waited, but he didn't say anything. I caught Maggie's eye. "How about a lift back to town?"

"Okay, but take it easy. Your engine's about to throw a rod."

"Town gossip, my cousin's hula hoop." I held the door for her. She went through it beaming.

21

"How come a nice-looking young fellow like you isn't married?"

We were making our way down the private road toward the car, stepping carefully to avoid slipping. It had rained even harder here than in Detroit; water plopped from the trees and last year's maple leaves plastered the muddy surface, shining like freshly spilled oil. Early mosquitoes squealed about but didn't bite. I hesitated before answering. She took my silence for reticence.

"Excuse my large mouth," she said. "I'm in my dotage."

"The hell you are. I was just wondering what made you think I'm not married."

"Ask me a hard one. You don't wear a wedding ring, and we've been together now—what?—two hours and you haven't even mentioned wanting to call your wife. You're not, are you?"

"Not recently."

"I guess you'd rather not talk about it."

"There aren't any rathers either way. I knew a cop once, a hard guy. The punks on his beat used to take their drugs and prostitutes and floating crap games to other neighborhoods when he came on duty. He got shot once while chasing a stickup artist down a blind alley, but he kept on running until he caught up with him. His partner found him ten minutes later, pale from loss of blood but still holding the guy pinned by the throat to a brick wall, waiting. Like

I said, he was a hard guy. But then he got married and had a couple of kids, and he wasn't so hard anymore. The punks started noising around what they'd do to his family if he didn't turn his back to this or that. Eventually his wife died from something or other and the kids grew up and moved out, but by then it was too late. Things got so bad on his beat he was forced into early retirement."

"What'd he do finally?"

"He took on a partner and went private. One day, he and the partner were shadowing this philandering husband as he was leaving his mistress's apartment. Nothing scary, just a routine tail job. He was on the street and the partner was parked in a car across the way, half a block behind the husband's car. The husband must have recognized the car from before, because he tugged a gun out of his coat pocket suddenly and pointed it at the partner behind the wheel. The ex-cop hollered, and the guy swung around and plugged him. Dead. He didn't even have his own gun with him; didn't think he'd need it. He'd forgotten how to be a hard guy."

"What happened to the husband?"

"The partner winged him through the car window and got out and took his gun away and called the police and an ambulance, in that order. It didn't seem right not to call for the ambulance, even though it wasn't needed."

"Don't tell me," she said. "You were the partner."

I didn't answer. "The husband pleaded diminished capacity and got off. He and his wife reconciled and are living in a condo in Florida. He grows roses. Every year on the anniversary of the shooting they get a picture postcard of Detroit in the mail. No message, just the picture."

The gate stood open, the chain broken and dangling. We reached the Cutlass and climbed in. I had to readjust the bucket seat to keep my knees out of my nostrils. Something rattled when I started the engine. She was right about the loose rod.

"Where's this logging trail you told me about?" I asked.

"The other side of that hill, I think. But it hasn't been

152

passable for some time. The lumber company's strung chains across both entrances.''

It was a steep hill like all the rest of them in that country, guttered along the aprons and blistered with white gravel stones that had washed down from the crest. I had the car up to forty at the base, but by the time we reached the top the engine was straining and the tires were grabbing only every third revolution. The loose rod clattered angrily. When we had surmounted the rise at last and were coasting down the other side, Maggie observed, ''I think that's an excuse.''

''What's an excuse?'' I tapped the brakes gently, on, off, on, off. This place must have been hell in January.

''That story about your partner. I'll bet it keeps most people from pressing you on why you don't get married.''

''Most of them.'' We hit a hole that snapped my teeth together.

''My guess is you got burned once and you're afraid to go near the stove again.''

The Cutlass shuddered over the washboard surface. I fought the wheel to keep us from plunging into one of the steep ditches that flanked the descent. ''Just what I ordered,'' I said, as we approached the level. ''Freud's Handy Guide to Home Analysis. Do you throw in free Gestalt?''

She made no reply. We had stopped before a sandy road that vanished into thick brush, its surface pulverized by the passage of many heavy trucks. A galvanized chain hammocked across the mouth between two steel posts, a rust-bubbled KEEP OUT sign suspended from it. I got out to examine the setup. The chain had been looped through an eye in the left post and padlocked to another in the right. The surface of the lock, dull from exposure, bore glistening pocks left by several sharp blows from a heavy instrument. The marks had been made since last night's rain or they would have rusted over. The shackle had been sprung; the whole thing was just hanging together. There were fresh tread marks in the soft sand beyond, at least two sets of them. I strode back, leaned in through the driver's side door, and killed the engine. Then I looked at Maggie in the passenger's seat.

"Are you up to another hike?"

"It's unlocked, isn't it?" she said.

"More like smashed."

She sighed. "Well, I've already made a liar out of my BE RIGHT BACK sign." She started to get out.

"There's a gun in the glove compartment. Take it out and give it to me."

"No there isn't." She opened her purse and lifted out the Luger in its holster. I stared at her. "You didn't expect me to go out looking for a phone without it, did you? For all I knew the first door I knocked on might be the murderer's."

"Good God, what would you have done if we'd been arrested and searched?" I accepted the piece and checked the clip. It was still loaded. I snapped the holster in place on my belt.

"Giggled, mainly. No one's pawed me in years."

I ducked under the chain and held it up for her. She noticed the tread marks right away. The road climbed gently between tunneling trees, and though it had once been wide enough for broad-base trucks hauling mammoth logs, nature had since crowded in so that there was barely room for one passenger vehicle to pass. One set of tire tracks had all but obliterated the other.

A hard white glint of sunlight bouncing off metal showed through the trees as we rounded the last bend. At length we came upon Albert Gold's brown two-door buried in the bushes at the side of the road. The tread marks said it had been pushed off the throughway. There were other marks in the sand that looked as if they had been made with a piece of bush or a broken branch, an old Indian trick to disguise footprints. Aside from a few fresh scratches the car appeared undamaged.

The door on the driver's side was unlocked. There was nothing kicking around loose inside. The ashtray held loose change and was too clean ever to have been used for its original purpose. I opened the glove compartment. A

Michigan road map, Gold's registration and certificate of insurance, a first aid kit, a paperback spy thriller, the pages curled from reading, a plastic ice scraper with a piece broken off. And a Colt Woodsman automatic in a stiff leather holster.

I released the clip. Loaded full up. The barrel smelled of fresh oil and disuse. The poor dumb bastard hadn't even thought to take it with him into the house. I wiped it off and put it back. Then I wiped off everything else handy and climbed out.

Ignoring Maggie's questioning glance, I stood in the middle of the road and made a 360-degree turn to get a hinge at the scenery. From here you could just see the peak of the A-frame among the trees not four hundred yards away. To avoid footprints I returned to the grown-over apron and walked along the edge, looking down at the sandy surface. Gold had parked behind the other vehicle, which had preceded him, I didn't know by how much. Some attempt had been made to obliterate the impressions made by the tread, but a clear piece showed just behind where the car had crossed the tracks Gold's had made leaving the road. The diamond pattern was distinctive.

It wouldn't have held up in court, unless some irregularity in the tread could be matched to the tires. There were probably a thousand similar sets of tires in the Detroit area alone. I had no legal reason to be standing there thinking that the design was very like that of the tires I had seen on Jack Billings's Trans Am back at the DeLancey estate.

22

I DIDN'T SAY ANYTHING TO MAGGIE ABOUT MY SUSPI-
cions. I hardly trusted them myself. On our way back down
I dragged a broken branch behind us to cover the footprints
we had made both ways. It wouldn't discourage a blind
Apache, but it felt good to do it.

"I suppose we should tell Hardacre about what we
found," she ventured when we were back in the car and
rolling toward town.

"They'll come across it soon enough. Cops aren't dumb,
except for their sense of humor." I drove for a while in
silence. Then: "What do you know about the last person
who rented the house?"

She turned a puzzled expression on me. Then she settled
back in the seat and frowned at the windshield. "It's been
so long. Months."

"Work on it. You haven't failed me yet."

"I don't think he ever came into the office and I never
heard his name," she said. "Mr. Kitchner, the owner of
the house, pointed him out to me once, on the street. Medium height, I guess, around forty. No older. He wasn't
the kind whose age you could guess easily. Slim, dark hair.
That's as much as I can dredge up short of hypnosis."

"Clothes? Complexion? What about his voice? Speech?
Any accent?"

"I never heard him speak. He dressed casually, like just
about everyone else around here. I don't remember any suit
or tie. Complexion?" Her brow furrowed. "Now that you

mention it, he had a very deep tan and his face was very smooth. It shone, in fact. It was his only distinctive feature, and I probably wouldn't have noticed it if it weren't wintertime.''

"It sounds like he was very good at being inconspicuous.''

"Do you think he's mixed up in this somehow?''

"I don't know," I said, exasperated. "It's just one of those things you ask, like who was the last person to see the deceased alive. Most of the time it doesn't amount to a damn. How long did he stay?''

"Not long. A week, maybe. He never came into town except to buy groceries and pick up a Detroit paper. He'd been gone a while when Kitchner died.''

"Where can I find Kitchner's widow?''

"In town. She lives with her daughter and son-in-law. The house is right on our way; I'll show it to you. I'd go in with you, but I've got an afternoon baseball game to cover. Worse luck.''

She pointed out a narrow, two-story house on a side street off the main drag and just inside the viaduct. It looked a hundred years old and probably was all of that and then some. I kept going and pulled up alongside a fire hydrant in front of the *Herald* office. Maggie gathered up her purse.

"Don't forget your promise.''

I nodded. "Noon Wednesday.''

"That's tomorrow.'' She got out and swung the door shut. The last I saw of her she was standing in the alcove in front of the office door looking for her keys.

A pinched-looking woman with watery blue eyes and hair bleached too light for her complexion answered my knock. I gave her my card and asked to speak with Mrs. Kitchner.

"What about?'' she asked, after reading the card. Her tone reeked of suspicion.

"The last man who rented Mr. Kitchner's house in the woods. He may be involved with an investigation I'm conducting.''

"Would this have anything to do with the call we got a little while ago from the sheriff's department?"

I said it would.

"Are you connected with the sheriff?"

I said I wasn't.

"I'm sorry, I can't let you speak to her. My mother had a coronary six weeks ago. Talking takes too much out of her. Besides, she wouldn't be much help. Old age has affected her mind as well as her body. She just lays there."

"I'd just like to ask her a couple of questions. It wouldn't take five minutes."

"I'm sorry. We don't let her have any visitors."

"None?"

"None." She started to close the door.

"Does she have a doctor?"

The question made her pause. The door remained open just wide enough for me to see her pinched face. "Yes," she said, as if she wasn't sure.

"Bet his bills are hard on the family budget."

She pressed her lips together. In small towns they still value privacy. I drew out my wallet.

"Would twenty dollars ease the blow?"

She looked at the twenty, then at me. The lines around her narrow mouth were as hard as graphite. "Your card says you're from Detroit," she snapped. "I'm not surprised. Maybe you can handle most folks there with money, but not here. Good-bye." The door banged in its casing.

I stood there a moment longer, still holding the double sawbuck. Then I returned it to the wallet and slipped the wallet back inside my jacket and stepped off the porch. I paused with my hand on the Cutlass door handle, looking at the second story of the house. Heavy curtains were drawn over one of the windows. I felt empty, but not as empty as the old woman lying up there, staring at the ceiling and waiting. I got in and drove back to the city.

NO ONE TOUCHES MY ENGINE BUT A SIXTY-TWO-YEAR-OLD German who runs a garage on Mack. He had installed it himself at cost, after the Coup de Ville from which it had come was totaled in a four-car pile-up on Eight Mile Road. He gave me hell for not coming to him sooner with that loose rod and told me to bring it in tomorrow afternoon, once he had finished making a serviceable Lincoln out of two Continentals that had gotten smashed up in separate accidents on the same day. I rated discounts for having helped spring his nephew from a Grand Theft Auto rap two years ago. The nephew was guilty as Cain, but I needed a good mechanic. From there I headed back downtown.

There were no visitors in my office. I collapsed into the chair behind the desk and massacred the office bottle. I felt like a handful of pocket lint. When the glass came up empty a second time I put the bottle back in the drawer and called the DeLancey house. The maid informed me that Mr. Billings was still on his way to Hawaii. I asked her if he had taken his car to the airport. She said he had. I thanked her and hung up. I sat there for a moment, pushing my lower lip in and out like Nero Wolfe. It didn't help.

The report on Janet Whiting was still in the desk. It didn't look to have been disturbed, so maybe Fitzroy and Cranmer hadn't tried to get a warrant after all. I paged through it absent-mindedly, without focusing on what was written there. I was thinking about what I had learned in Huron and what I hadn't, adding them up in two separate columns and arriving with two separate zeros. A fisherman like the late Judge might have called it trolling without bait.

Suddenly I stopped paging. The bound report flipped shut of its own weight. Outside the window and three stories down, someone stood on his brakes in the middle of the street, his tires shrieking like a dog caught in a meat grinder. I barely heard it. After a long moment I lifted the receiver with a quaking hand and called Phil Montana's office. Bill Clendenan answered.

"Is he in?"

He recognized my voice. There was a pause during which I heard "The Shadow of Your Smile" being drawn from syrupy strings in the background.

"Listen, Walker—" he began.

"I heard it. The bass fiddle needs tuning. Just tell him

159

I'll be around in a little while. Tell him I think I know who killed Bingo Jefferson and why. Tell him I've got an idea who did in Krim and that I'm pretty sure about the identity of the one responsible for a third murder he doesn't know anything about. Tell him that.''

He didn't answer for five or six bars. Then:

"Is that all?'' His tone was icily ironic.

"Not quite,'' I said. "You can also tell him I think Judge Arthur DeLancey's still alive.''

I rung off before he could react.

23

A CROWD OF ABOUT TWENTY WORKERS IN CAPS AND
Windbreakers was boiling around the parking lot entrance
to the RenCen, homemade picket signs thrashing above
their heads. STRIKE NOW! screamed one in red Magic
Marker letters. Another bellowed OPEN YOUR EYES, PHIL!
and still another, STEELERS VS. STEALERS. A handful of
sweating police officers in uniform stood on the fringes,
trying to get the pickets moving in an orderly circle. The
air was brittle with tension.

"Hey!"

A squat man whose jacket sleeves were rolled past mus-
cular bronze forearms, the left a couple of shades darker
than the right, inserted his hard round belly in front of the
steps as I approached, blocking my path. I backed up a
couple of paces and bumped into two more standing behind
me.

"You going up to see Phil Montana?" demanded the
first.

I took my time answering. His broad face, originally
white, was burned dark and cracked at the corners of his
eyes and lips. He had cigar breath. He was at least four
inches shorter than I, but he had forty pounds on me easy,
none of them soft. The guys behind me were my height
and no less solid.

"If I told you I was, would you take to your bed and
sulk?"

"One of us might end up in bed," he grunted. "But it wouldn't be me and the bed would be in a hospital."

He had a United Steelhaulers patch on his Windbreaker. "I thought you union boys were all for Montana."

"We are. Which is why we're doing this, to get his attention. He's been listening to the men around him too long. He don't talk to the rank and file no more. We figure we can set him straight on how they're selling us down the river to the big mills."

"I get it. When no one comes up to see him he'll come down to find out why."

"Yeah, that's it."

"It won't work. He'll just send one of his stooges down here in his place. Or have the cops break it up."

"Then there'll be some heads busted. Right, boys?"

Assent rumbled through the crowd. One of the workers, a big black, slung his picket sign over one shoulder and hooked a thumb inside the watch pocket of his jeans, spreading his jacket to reveal the soldered end of a lead pipe sticking above the waistband.

"So I'm asking you again," said the spokesman. "Is your business with Montana or ain't it?"

"Hell, don't look at me. I'm just an insurance agent. You want to buy a policy?" I produced a card from my collection, identifying me as Sherman Brady of the Midwest Confidential Life, Automobile & Casualty Company. He made a face and stepped aside to let me pass. Like I said, you never know when they may come in handy.

This time the secretary himself was waiting for me when I stepped off the elevator. He was wearing a different tan suit, this one a shade lighter. He wasn't smoking. The two plainclothes bodyguards loomed bigger than ever behind him.

"I told him," Clendenan said. "He's waiting."

I was frisked again and showed empty. The uniformed guard didn't look up from his desk as we passed him. "Camelot" was tootling out of the speakers above the male clerical staff, hard at work as usual. An image flashed through my mind of a world in ruins, a mushroom cloud

162

spreading over the rubble, and one lone speaker at the top of a twisted pole, playing one empty tune after another until the electricity ran out.

Montana's door stood open. The boss sat at his desk, fingering his World Series baseball and pretending to read the signatures on the horsehide. The desk was clear of paperwork. Blocky and solid-looking as before, he also looked tired. He had a jacket on this time and was wearing eyeglasses with half-lenses. I stood before him while Clendenan closed the door from outside.

After a while he leaned back in his swivel chair and returned the ball to its place on the shelf. Then he folded his hands across his spare middle and looked at me over the top of his glasses. He inclined his head abruptly toward the chair I had occupied during my last visit. I accepted it.

"You can start with why you think Arthur's still alive," he said.

I was in the act of lighting a cigarette. I drew the smoke as far down as it would go, shook out the match, and leaned over to drop it into a square black onyx ashtray on the edge of the desk. I squirted smoke.

"I don't have any evidence that he is," I began. "Just a hunch. But it's a hell of a hunch.

"He had tax problems, big tax problems. The kind that can land a man in a cell for a long time no matter how important he is. There was only one way out of it: to disappear. But disappearing isn't as easy as it was once. First you need money, a lot of it if you want to continue living the way the Judge did. So he set up a dummy company, Griffin Carbide. He got his friends to invest in it on the rumor that it was going to merge with a bigger company. It didn't and it folded. His friends took the loss. Only it didn't fold, on account of I found out today that it owns property thirty miles west of here. I figure DeLancey's been drawing on Griffin's funds since his vanishing act, just as if it were his personal bank account. The ready cash he needed to start came from selling his firearms collection outright to his stepson, Jack Billings.

"His scenario was just flashy enough to be believed.

163

Everyone knew how keen he was on fishing and the outdoors, so he arranged an excursion to Canada over Lake Superior. To make it look like a working vacation he invited his aide. Then at the last minute he bowed out. Probably he claimed pressing business and told the pilot and aide to go ahead and he'd meet them later, traveling by automobile around the lake. Only they never made it across Superior. Maybe he tampered with the engine, maybe he planted some kind of bomb. It doesn't matter. What matters is the plane went down over the most treacherous body of water on earth. As far as the public and anyone else were concerned, the Judge went down with it.''

I paused to draw on my cigarette and give Montana a chance to comment. He didn't. He was staring at his strong square hands resting on his stomach. I continued.

''It was a peach of a setup. He didn't confide in anyone, not even his family or mistress. It was almost perfect except that he didn't count on his late pilot having a brother.

''The pilot went by the name of Collins, but according to DeLancey's chauffeur his real handle was Krim, the same as the Arab who owned The Crescent. I've seen Collins's picture and the family resemblance is unmistakable. Krim—the Krim of The Crescent—had a substantial bank balance and was in the habit of making regular deposits in large amounts. Somehow he found out that the Judge wasn't on that plane when his brother went swimming, and his revenge took a lucrative turn. It's my guess he used the blood money he squeezed out of DeLancey to buy the joint on Cass, which made a good front should the IRS start wondering where he derived his income. I bet if you look it up you'll find that Griffin Carbide is a major investor. But what Krim was getting was scrapings compared to what DeLancey had to draw on, so everyone was happy. Then Janet Whiting showed up.

''She was bitter about the disappearance of the Judge's last will and determined to find it. Somewhere along the way she tumbled to Krim's relationship to DeLancey and became an employee at The Crescent under an assumed name to learn more. You found out she was working there

164

and because you felt responsible for her—later we'll go over just why—you sent Bingo Jefferson down to look after her.''

"I told you that," put in Montana.

I nodded. "But you didn't tell me that you fathered her illegitimate child back in Huron—which, the laws governing paternity suits being what they are, was a good enough motive to send Jefferson not to protect her, but to kill her.''

He stopped staring at his hands and leveled his gaze at me. For an instant I was transported back to a jungle in Southeast Asia, face to face with a guerrilla I'd stumbled across with his hands buried in the bloody face of a writhing G.I. I'd had my M-16 with me, and it had all been over in a second. But I never forgot his eyes. I made a gesture of dismissal.

"Relax, I wasn't accusing you. If you'd wanted her on ice you would have put her there long ago. Fatherhood is just as strong a motive for feeling *protective* toward the woman involved. Unfortunately, she didn't see it that way, and when she spotted Jefferson—a menacing enough figure at the best of times—she got nervous and called me. Remember, she couldn't be sure that you weren't in on the plot.''

"What makes you think I'm not?''

"An investigator survives on hunches. If you'd been that kind of a guy you would never have stood trial on that chintzy assault rap, let alone been convicted. You'd have fixed it. I'm rambling.

"Jefferson eavesdropped on my conversation with Janet Whiting—or Ann Maringer, as I knew her. He saw the ring change hands, figured out what it represented, and tried to get it back from me because he knew it would make trouble if it was traced back to you. You know what came of that. After I left and Janet got off work he followed her to her apartment. He had to find out where the ring went. He backed her into the bedroom, where she snatched a gun from somewhere and shot him. Or maybe not.

"Maybe someone else followed her home. Someone like Krim, who had grown suspicious and was afraid she was

165

going to spoil his good thing. Maybe he shot Jefferson and grabbed the woman to use as an extra bargaining point with DeLancey. Somewhere there's a thirty-two derringer floating around that may have been what did the job on your bodyguard. It's the ideal murder weapon—unregistered, untraceable, and easy to hide. Don't ask me how he got it; I'm hypothesizing. Why Krim died and who did it is still up in the air, but I'm betting the Judge was in no mood for further squeezing.''

Montana said, ''You mentioned another murder.''

I blew a jet of smoke at a corner of the ceiling. Beyond the window the Detroit skyline was limned in a haze of blue smog under a layer of dying sunshine. ''You may read about it in tonight's paper,'' I said. ''The local media people like to play up violent crimes that happen in other places. About noon a young Reliance Investigations operative named Albert Gold was gutshot and left for dead in the house you used to rent outside Huron. He left a terrible mess on his way downstairs. Later his car was found shoved off an abandoned logging road not far away. Tread marks found at the scene indicate that another car had been parked on the road when Gold arrived. I think they were left by a car belonging to Jack Billings.

''Billings supplied me with a report on Janet Whiting that his mother had commissioned Reliance to prepare. He had substituted a page in the background section in order to throw me off the track, and went to Huron. I don't know why. Maybe he thought Janet Whiting was stashed there. Maybe he suspected his stepfather was still alive and, like Krim, saw a profit in it. Or maybe that sappy story he tried to sell me about being infatuated with Janet was true after all. Anyway he went there, and not long afterward so did Gold.

''His motives are easier to figure. You'll remember I asked if you knew who was tailing me earlier. It was Gold, one of the operatives who had been keeping you under surveillance for the steel mills.''

''I had the office checked out after you tipped me,'' Montana said. ''The telephones had been tapped and the office wired. We're suing Reliance for invasion of privacy."

"Good for you. Gold tried to shake me down after he saw me coming out of The Crescent, where Krim was killed. By bugging our last conversation he learned who Ann Maringer is. It's my guess he got hold of his agency's file on Janet Whiting and that greed brought him out to Huron. There he tangled with Billings and fell down hard."

"Interesting," he commented, after a short silence, during which I finished my cigarette and rubbed it out in the onyx tray. "And quite plausible, granting the original supposition that Arthur isn't dead. But why come to me with it?"

"I thought you might be able to fill in some of the gaps. Such as what really happened out there twenty-four years ago, and what it has to do with anything."

There was another pause, and then his lips smiled thinly, wholly independent of the rest of his face. "Detectives. Everything always has to have something to do with something else. Don't you recognize coincidence?"

"You're stalling."

"Damn right I'm stalling. I don't think as fast on my feet as I used to. It might interest you to know that Janet Whiting never bore my child, and that we never had sex before my wife died and Arthur DeLancey disappeared."

I made myself more comfortable in my chair. "It might."

He leaned back again and rescued the beat-up baseball from the shelf. This time he didn't finger it. He placed it in the center of the desk and proceeded to ignore it.

"I was living there at that time, in that rented house in the woods," he admitted. "Under an assumed name, for the sake of privacy. It was my first vacation in years. I met Janet in the local hardware store. She saw that I was buying fishing tackle, recognized a trout lure in my purchase, and mentioned a pond where the trout were biting. Apparently she was something of a tomboy, and not at all shy of strangers, though she could barely bring herself to give her order to the clerk, who she must have known for years. I

167

was never much of a fisherman, but I was interested for the sake of my house guest, who was. She offered to show me the way. I took her up on it.

"After we had driven out there I invited her up to the house for lunch. Don't look at me that way, Walker; it was a hot day and I was happily married. What I forgot—"

"—was that DeLancey wasn't," I finished. "He was your guest, wasn't he?"

He glared. "If you knew that, why'd you insist I was mixed up with her back then?"

"I wanted to hear you say it. I wasn't sure you would if I didn't jolt it out of you. The Judge had to have been there. It came to me when I got back to town this afternoon. He was the fisherman in this case, not you."

"You know what's wrong with you, Walker? You're too damned circumspect for your own good. One of these days you're going to zigzag yourself into a real jam." His eyes dropped to the baseball on his desk and his expression softened. I wondered what it was about that ball. He continued in a quieter voice.

"Arthur took one look at Janet that day and something came into his eyes I didn't like. But he was too smart to try anything while I was around. Nothing happened that day."

"Nothing?"

"Not a thing. She had eaten and was about to leave when the police came. Her father was with them, red-faced and mad as hell. I've battered men who called me worse than he did, but he was a man with a half-grown daughter and I was in the wrong."

"Didn't the cops ask for identification?"

"I had a phony driver's license made out in the name of Peter Martin, an alias. You have to appreciate the occasional need for privacy in my work. Anyway, it satisfied them. Arthur was out fishing at that time; no one saw him. They took the girl away and that was the end of it. I thought.

"Arthur was good-looking in those days. Women were always ready to fall in love with him, and he was a spoiled

168

little kid when it came to self-discipline. He couldn't control his urges. I figured Janet was too young to have those kinds of thoughts, but kids were getting to be a lot older than I was at the same age. It was a week before I found out that instead of going fishing, Arthur had been meeting the girl in the woods. He said she came to him the first time he visited the pond, and that it had got to be a regular thing. He said it was her eyes that attracted him, which I could believe. She had—has—beautiful eyes, bluer than any I ever saw.

"I blew my top. I told him to pack up and get the hell out of my house. He did, and I cleared out right afterward. I wasn't going to be around when her old man found out what had been going on."

"Is that why you and the Judge split up?"

"I suppose it played a part, but not right away. Later, much later, I found out that the girl's family had come to Detroit when they found out she was pregnant. I tried to get in touch with her, but he—I'm assuming it was her father's decision—wanted nothing to do with me. I never saw Janet again until she took up with DeLancey years later. By that time she was a woman and old enough to make her own decisions. Her father was dead. I was no longer involved."

He looked at me hard. "That's it, except that I felt responsible again after Arthur disappeared and left her without a cent. The son she had raised alone was old enough to work. I gave him a job here. I think my affair with Janet grew out of that. So you can see why I care what happens to her. She bought a piece of me twenty-four years ago and I'm still paying interest on the mortgage."

"Noble."

"Far from it. I won't say I didn't get something out of the relationship. Janet had changed a great deal in the years since Huron. There she was awkward, unsure of herself. As a woman she was poised and graceful, if not exactly beautiful. Her maturity had caught up with her early dancing lessons. I was proud to have won her, if only for a little while."

169

"So it was Griffin Carbide that ended your friendship with DeLancey."

"That again," he said impatiently. "Yes. I was never able to prove it, but I suspected from the beginning that he manipulated that stock for his own benefit. It wasn't the money, even though it took a big bite out of funds belonging to the men I was elected to represent. It was the fact that he'd cheat the organization that made him. That I can't forgive. If you're right, and he's living off what he stole from this union, I'll use whatever influence I have left to make sure he spends what's left of his life inside walls."

I frowned at the ruled notepad upon which I had been recording his statement. Then I met his gaze. "I'd like to meet Janet Whiting's son."

"You already have." He turned to the intercom on his desk, and I noticed for the first time that the orange light was shining on the panel, which meant that every word we'd said had been heard in the outer office. "Bill, come in here."

24

BILL CLENDENAN CAME IN LIKE A MAN WALKING THROUGH a neighborhood he used to know well but didn't trust anymore—high on the balls of his feet, sidling as if to present a narrower target. He had his right hand inside the flap pocket of his jacket.

Montana said, "Bill, relax. You checked out Walker yourself. You know he's into no one but himself."

"That doesn't mean I have to like him," snapped the other. "He's got a lot of smart mouth."

I had stood to face him. We were about the same height. "You're Janet Whiting's son?"

"And Arthur DeLancey's. Not that he ever acknowledged it, even in private." He fingered the object in his pocket idly. It didn't make much of a bulge. I figured it for a small-caliber weapon, possibly a .25. Not that the size of the bore mattered much at this distance.

"I knew there was something familiar about you. She raised you?"

"As best she could, under the circumstances. You grow up fast when you have to spend three nights a week on the streets while your mother's home entertaining."

He spat the last word. I said, "DeLancey wouldn't help?"

"She never asked him for anything. He never even knew she was living in Detroit until they happened to meet at a taxi stand. That's when she picked up where they had left off. She had to. I was in jail on a breaking and entering rap and she needed the money to raise bail. Even then, he was the one who made the offer. He thought he was buying her a new wardrobe. A man like Judge Arthur DeLancey couldn't be seen with a part-time whore in bargain basement clothes.''

"Don't talk about her like that!" Montana snarled.

"Who's the gun for?" I asked.

The union chief started. He seemed to notice his secretary's hidden hand for the first time. "Take that damn thing out of your pocket! All I need is you getting pinched for carrying a concealed weapon. I'm trying to change this union's image, not propagate it.''

"Call it an heirloom. Handed down to me by my beloved father.'' He took out the hand, revealing a one-shot derringer in his palm.

It was the Forehand & Wadsworth that Billings had told me about, a cheap belly gun cranked out by the hundreds between 1870 and the turn of the century. The nickel plating had worn down to dull steel in spots, and the ivory grip was as yellow as horses' teeth. It was scarcely longer than a man's index finger. But it could kill. So could a man's index finger, for that matter.

I put out my hand and he gave it to me, just like that. I sniffed the barrel. It smelled of fresh oil, like vanilla extract. I found the release, pivoted the barrel, and tapped out the cartridge. It was a modern centerfire, which this model was equipped to handle. I pointed the pistol toward the window and peered inside the barrel. No dust. It had been cleaned and oiled recently. I replaced the cartridge and rolled the barrel back into place.

"I'll hold onto this for now, if you don't mind," I told Clendenan, putting it in my pocket. "You don't look like the sort of man who's used to carrying a gun around. Where's your father?"

"This is news to me." Montana was standing behind his desk with his hands flat on the top, staring at his secretary. "Why didn't you tell me he was still alive and that you knew where he was?"

Clendenan stared back. "I didn't trust you. I didn't trust

anyone. Especially not him." His eyes flicked in my direction, then back to his employer.

"Maybe you trust the police." I took a step toward the desk, reaching for the telephone.

"Try calling them with two broken arms."

The secretary's voice was hoarse with warning. It made me hesitate. Hard knots showed at the corners of his jaw.

"Who are you going to get to do it?" demanded Montana. "Not my bodyguards. They take their orders from me."

"Is that what you think?" Clendenan crossed in front of me, leaned over the desk and flipped on the intercom, which Montana had turned off. "Okay."

The bodyguards entered, the one wearing glasses in front. They closed the door and took up positions on either side of it, their hands folded before them. Except for the Ivy League look they might have stepped off a B-movie set. Every once in a while Hollywood nails it square on the nose.

The union chief tore off his own glasses with a savage gesture. "What the hell is this? I didn't call you in here. Get back outside where you belong!"

Neither of them moved.

The secretary smirked. "I spend more time with them than you do. One of the disadvantages of being dedicated and locking yourself in the office twelve hours at a stretch. The eight months you spent in stir helped. They take your pay, but they take mine too, and more of it. You're always asking me why I need such a large expense account. Now you know."

Montana ignored him. He stalked from behind his desk and confronted the bespectacled guard, glaring up at the man, who towered nearly a foot above him. "I told you to get out."

A brief look passed between the guard and Clendenan. Suddenly a huge hand lashed out and Montana went reeling. The guard hadn't moved another muscle, just his forearm. But his employer had to clutch at the edge of the desk with both hands to keep from falling. The right side of his

173

face was red, and he was wheezing like an asthmatic. I suddenly realized that he wasn't healthy.

"You're always saying that the public is afraid of violence." His secretary's voice was taunting. "That it's the brutal few and not the meek that will inherit the earth. You'll be happy to know I haven't forgotten a thing you taught me."

"I treated you like a son," gasped the other. He was staring at the battered and discolored object on his desk, scribbled over with names like Kaline and Freehan and Northrup and Lolich, names that rang no longer from loudspeakers on sunny days where men gathered to play ball before cheering crowds.

Clendenan laughed harshly. "Why? Because I once gave you a moth-eaten souvenir of a dead baseball team for Father's Day? Or to salve your conscience because of what happened in Huron? The only father I'm interested in is my real one. He's got millions. He's no washed-up jailbird. Show him, Tim."

The other guard, slimmer than his partner, towheaded and freckling at the tops of his cheeks, tugged a big automatic from inside his coat and covered the room. In his hand the Army Colt looked like a lady's purse gun. Clendenan held out his hand.

"The derringer, Walker. Carrying guns is like eating peanuts, hard to give up."

I fished it out carefully and watched him return it to his own pocket. "Shall I wrap us up, or will you kill us here?" I asked.

"Always the card. No one's going to be killed if I can help it. You're getting your wish, to meet the late Judge DeLancey. And my mother."

"They're together?" Montana had managed to pull himself upright, though he continued to use the desk as support. His color was returning in patches, under a sheen of perspiration. "Where?"

"At my house. The one you bought for me in Grosse Ile. I assume you want to accompany us out there. I'm no kidnaper."

I indicated the towhead's .45. "What's that, a corsage?"

The secretary smiled wearily. "Like the farmer said, 'First you got to get his attention.' Okay, Tim."

The automatic returned to its hiding place beneath the bodyguard's left arm.

"Just don't forget he has it," warned Clendenan. "Let's go."

The staff hardly glanced at us as we passed through the outer office, Montana in the middle of a flying wedge made up of his secretary, the guards, and me. If anyone noticed that the boss looked a little under the weather, none reacted. The uniformed guard got up to hold the door open for us. No one said anything in the elevator on the way down.

The situation in the parking lot was still simmering as we emerged from the building. The gang of steelhaulers spotted us and crowded in tightly, shouting to attract Montana's attention. They made "Phil" sound like a royal title. The harried cops moved in to clear a path.

My eyes met those of the blocky leader just before Tim shouldered him into the waiting arms of a husky young officer with a walrus moustache. To my back he snarled, "Sell him a policy yet?"

"What's that about?" Clendenan wanted to know. We kept moving, striding swiftly through the momentary opening in the wall of humanity.

"Mistaken identity," I replied.

We waited in the aisle while Tim brought around our wheels, a midnight blue Cadillac limousine with blacked-out windows and a finish like patent leather. With both guards up front there was room enough for the three of us and a bowling alley in the deep back seat. There was a telephone in the car and a portable bar.

"Where do you keep the stewardess?" I asked. "In the glove compartment?"

"You've got wit, shamus. What you lack is timing." The secretary watched the scenery slide by the window as

175

Tim wheeled us expertly through the lot and out onto Jefferson.

We turned west, where the street lights were just coming on. The sun was below the Detroit skyline. Tim turned on the heater against the gathering chill. It hissed softly, like snakes in a barrel.

"Why the tour?" I reached for a Winston and came up with an empty pack. Clendenan offered me one of his. Kools. I accepted it resignedly and lit up.

"To get you off my back. I've seen enough to know you don't stop rooting around until you've uncovered something. This way maybe you won't do so much damage."

"That stinks."

He shrugged and watched the buildings go by.

"How'd you get the gun away from DeLancey?" I sucked hard on the coffin nail, but it still tasted like the cotton that dentists stuff into the mouths of helpless patients.

"He gave it to me."

I said, "I guess I'm trying to come up with a clever way to get you to tell me the whole story."

"Krim took the derringer away from the Judge when he tried to threaten him out of his blackmail scheme." He continued to gaze out the window. "DeLancey—you'll excuse me if I don't call him Father—wasn't so good at killing when he was face to face with his intended victim. The Arab held onto it because an unregistered firearm can be a useful item. He had it with him the night he followed Bingo Jefferson to my mother's apartment, and used it to kill him when he figured the bodyguard had too much education. Mother had a gun, too, but Krim had another, a thirty-two automatic, and it didn't take long to disarm her.

"DeLancey was staying in an apartment in Troy, where he'd moved from the house he'd been living in under another name out West since his disappearance. There were rumors that the IRS was about to nose into Griffin Carbide's affairs, wondering why the business was still making investments five years after it filed for bankruptcy; he came back to juggle all the company's holdings into several other

176

dummy firms he'd set up at the same time, just in case. He thought if he tangled things further, not even the computers would be able to sort them out. Krim stashed Mother with him, along with a reminder that if she got away, everything would be out in the open. DeLancey agreed. He had assistants, of course, though none of them knew their employer's real name. By now they're halfway to Peru. They cut and run the minute Krim bellied up dead. Let me know if I'm lapping you.''

"So far I'm still in the race." I glanced at Montana on the other side of me. He was staring at the pile carpeting between the front and back seats.

"Krim thought he had them both buffaloed," he continued, pausing only to fire up a cigarette for himself with the aid of a throwaway butane lighter. "He even boasted of killing Jefferson, knowing that neither DeLancey nor my mother could go to the law, as he couldn't risk exposing himself and she was wanted in connection with the murder. He wasn't even suspicious the next day when the Judge came to see him at The Crescent, supposedly to meet his latest blackmail demand. He was contemptuous enough to turn his back while he opened the cash box to salt away the money. He didn't know his visitor was carrying a claw hammer, the ideal murder weapon if the police were to believe it was the work of a strung-out hophead looking for a score. He probably didn't even feel it crush his skull.

"That ended that threat, but DeLancey didn't count on the murder hitting the headlines so heavily, or on his flunkies panicking and clearing out, letting my mother escape. The Judge wasn't anyone's fool, though. He knew there was only one person in the city she felt she could trust not to betray her, and looked me up. She wasn't at my place an hour before he crashed in waving that silly derringer.''

The limousine cruised through DelRay, a populous community of workers once known as Boneville, when the Michigan Carbon Works started taking in tons of buffalo bones in 1881, following the great slaughter out West. The air in the car began to stink despite the sealed windows. We were passing Zug Island, that 325-acre toilet occupied by Great Lakes Steel and Allied Chemical, spiny with smokestacks belching great columns of toxic waste into the air daily. On the opposite side of the car, farther away, an eerie, surrealistic glow reddened the bellies of low-hanging clouds and the sluggish surface of the River Rouge, a garish reminder that Ford continues to make cars while the rest of the world shakes itself apart. It was a weird sight, like St. Elmo's fire illuminating a ship at sea.

The smell was overpowering, and not all of it was coming from the plants.

I put out my cigarette in the recessed ashtray behind the front seat. "So how come you're here to tell me all this? And how'd you find out what went before?"

"My mother told me. Some of it she got from DeLancey and she figured out the rest. As to why I'm not lying somewhere with a hole in me, you'll see when we get there."

I looked at him, at his profile sliding in and out of focus as we passed between street lights. The orange tip of his cigarette flew to his lips, brightened, then faded again as he lowered it and returned his attention to the street. He was drawing inward again. I wondered if that had anything to do with the growing nearness of his parents. His parents. The phrase seemed mundane for the situation.

"Where'd you get the name Clendenan?"

"It's my middle name. It belonged to my great-grandmother. I was born Bill Whiting. I dropped it in a fit of shame for my mother's lifestyle. I've gotten over being ashamed, but it's too late to change back."

"Where's she been the past year?"

"Who knows? I suspect out West, tracing my father. When he came back so did she. I don't know why. She raised me, she loves me, but she's never confided in me."

"She seems to have told you plenty about what's happened lately."

"That's not the same thing."

The house was one of the fine old French homes located beyond the naval base on Grosse Ile, trimmed delicately with gingerbread and flanked on both sides by private sculptured gardens, miniatures of the grounds at Versailles, bathed in soft white light from hooded outdoor lamps set at ground level and complete with trees planted in bullet-straight rows and trimmed into upright cylinders. This would have been what Cadillac had in mind when he stepped ashore not six hundred yards away and said, "Here I shall build a city."

Of course, he wouldn't have counted on the man standing in the open doorway with a gun in his hand.

25

Silhouetted against the yellow oblong of lighted doorway, he was a man of medium height, trimly built, and wearing a light-colored shirt tucked into the tops of tight-fitting pants. His features were in shadow, but the large, nickel-plated revolver in his hand gleamed brightly in the glow of the garden lamps. He had caught us just as we were climbing out of the car. No one moved. Cars swished by on Jefferson, but they might as well have been a hundred miles off.

"Reach for the sky, sidewinders!"

His tone was an exaggerated guttural, rough as cactus. We complied, the two bodyguards leading the way. No one has more respect for firearms than a man who carries one regularly.

At that moment the porch light came on above his head. He stood blinking in its unexpected glare. His breath rode the frosty air in vapor. He had dark hair, thinning in front. His features were dominated by deep-set eyes and a wide mouth and the light shone off his medium tan. But something had gone wrong with his face.

The left side sagged as if gravity had gotten its hooks into his mouth and eyelids and was tugging downward with all its might. The arm on that side hung limply, and the way he leaned against the door jamb said that his left leg was just as useless. He'd dragged himself across the room. His hair and skin said he was forty, but his ravaged body was at least twenty years older. I might not have recognized him but for that, so completely had the dye job and face-lift altered the appearance of the man whose photographs I had studied earlier. He'd lost weight as well. He fit Maggie's description of the last man to rent the house near Huron.

Judge Arthur DeLancey was dressed in a white cowboy shirt with an ornate black yoke embroidered in gold. His Levi's were brand new, held up by a broad leather belt with a big square silver buckle, and hung stiff over square leather cowboy boots with two-inch heels, intricately tooled. The whole outfit was new, including the gun belt he was wearing, slung low and strapped down like in the movies, and the gun in his hand. Its mate was in the other holster near his dead arm. I shifted my stare from one firearm to the other. There was something . . .

"Come inside, Arthur." The voice, coming from behind the man in the doorway, was feminine, conciliatory, familiar. "It's too late to go out and play."

Too late to go out and play. Again I studied the object he was holding and the one he wasn't.

"Those aren't—"

Things got noisy then. A hoarse roar was followed by a crack as something sped past me too fast to see and struck DeLancey with a ripe thump. He dropped his gun, placed his good hand over his right eye in a clumsy salute, sobbed, and slid down the jamb, something dark staining his face. A high-pitched scream shredded the air. That's the part of it I still hear from time to time, the scream.

I turned around. Phil Montana was standing with one foot still inside the limousine, both arms stretched in front of him and with something smoking between his hands. His eyes were wide.

"You son of a bitch!" Clendenan, standing beside him and slightly in front, backhanded his boss, who sprawled against the side of the car, lost his balance, and went down hard on one knee in the driveway. The revolver he had been holding struck the asphalt, skidded under the Cadillac, bounded off a tire, and came to rest against my left foot.

All eyes were on Montana. I ducked swiftly and came up holding the gun behind my leg.

"That was a toy gun DeLancey had!" shrilled the secretary.

"God, my God!" The union chief lowered himself to a sitting position on the pavement. He ran shaking fingers through his stiff gray hair. "My God, I didn't know!"

Clendenan spun on the nearest of the two bodyguards, the one wearing glasses. "Why the hell didn't you frisk him before we left the office?"

The bodyguard looked hurt. "You didn't tell me to."

"Do I have to tell you everything, schmuck?"

I was watching Montana. "Where'd you get the piece?"

"I've carried one for twenty years, not counting the time in stir and my parole. Ever since some nut took a shot at me during a union rally. I used to have a permit. My God!" He was staring at the ground now, and rubbing his hands between his thighs. He looked like a big kid playing in a mud puddle.

More sobs were coming from the doorway. A woman was kneeling next to DeLancey's twitching body, cradling his shattered head in her lap and rocking back and forth. Janet Whiting. Ann Maringer. Something about the spasms running through the man's limbs said his problems were about over. It had taken five years for the plane crash to catch up with him. The bodyguards had their guns out now and had the woman covered, waiting for instructions from Clendenan.

"Find that gun," he told the towhead, jerking his chin in the direction of the Cadillac.

Tim grumbled something about just having gotten his suit back from the cleaners, holstered his .45, and got down on his hands and knees to peer under the car. I moved back a step.

"He had a stroke." Clendenan was watching the tableau in the doorway. "Not five minutes after he burst in looking for Mother. He collapsed, and when he finally came to, it was obvious that his brain was affected. Sometimes he's lucid. The rest of the time he's like a ten-year-old. I've been putting off calling a doctor. It would be all over the papers and TV if I did.''

I recognized the symptoms of shock and let him ramble on.

"We found a key to his apartment in one of his pockets, along with a paper with the Troy address written on it. That's where the outfit he's wearing came from. It had never been worn. Maybe he bought it as a joke, or to go with his new collection. I suppose you know that the old West was one of his hobbies. Dressing him that way calmed him down.''

"It isn't under there.'' Tim climbed to his feet and dusted off the knees of his trousers.

"Look on the other side,'' said the secretary.

While he was watching the bodyguard circle the car I slipped the revolver into the side pocket of my jacket and left it there with my hand around it. It felt like a .38. It was like coming home.

Tim came back. "It isn't there either.''

Clendenan said, "Keep looking. It's got to be somewhere.''

"I'm telling you it isn't.''

Three pairs of eyes—the secretary's and those of the two bodyguards—turned toward me. The one with glasses brought around his gun, a twin of his partner's .45. I showed him mine.

"Now that we've all got one, let's put them away and be friends,'' I suggested.

The bodyguard hesitated a beat, then glanced at his superior. The towhead was frozen in mid-step with his hands spread at his side. The air got still.

"This isn't necessary,'' Clendenan pointed out. "You aren't in any danger.''

"Not anymore.''

The bodyguard and the secretary exchanged fresh glances. They had communication down to a science. The automatic went into its holster. When the hand that had been holding it came back out empty I pocketed the .38 and stepped up onto the small front porch.

183

The woman was still cuddling the dying man and rocking, though the sobbing had stopped. She had on a cheap thin cotton dress and nothing underneath. The pattern was spoiled by a spreading stain—greasy black in the harsh overhead light—beneath the Judge's head. It was leaking from the place where his right eye had been. His breath came in short gulps. His lungs and heart hadn't heard he was dead.

I pulled a brown woolen blanket from a chair on the porch and draped it over her shoulders. She didn't acknowledge my presence. She looked old in that light, and drawn. Only her eyes remained bright and new. Lake Superior wasn't that blue on the clearest of days. Tears silvered her cheeks.

I went back and asked Clendenan for his pack of Kools. On my way back to the house I lit two, bent down and slid one between her lips. She accepted it without moving. But the glowing tip brightened and I knew she was smoking it.

"You're pretending deeper shock than you're in," I said gently. "I did a job for a shrink once. He told me about people with emotional problems. Mainly about how they like to exaggerate them."

"What do you know about it?"

She spoke emptily and sniffled, rather sloppily. I gave her my handkerchief. "What I don't know about the brain would fill Joe Louis Arena. Why don't we go inside and talk?"

"I don't want to leave him." She used the handkerchief to mop up the blood around his empty eye socket.

"It won't make any difference."

She jumped as if I'd slapped her. Oh, but I was a callous bastard. That was something else I had learned from the shrink, not to humor them when it was obvious they were faking. I hoped he was right. Just in case he wasn't I hedged my bet.

"Carry him inside," I told the bodyguards. To her: "Is there a couch or something we can lay him on?"

"Yes. Yes, there is. In the living room."

Neither of the gorillas had moved. "What are you waiting for, a resurrection?" I demanded.

Tim stuck out his chin. "Who elected you president?"

"Do what he said," advised the secretary.

It was a clumsy operation, the towhead trying to keep the blood off his suit while the guard in glasses handled the other end and the woman tried to follow along, holding the Judge's unresponsive hand. My stomach did a slow turn just watching them.

The house was decorated in quiet taste, whatever that is. The living room carpet was sculptured and held no footprints. The beige wallpaper went well with dark brown upholstered furniture, and suspended panels brought the ceiling down to a sensible height. Only one lamp was burning, which left the room's corners in deep shadow. Rumpled bedding and a dented pillow on the sofa showed where someone had been sleeping. Gently the reluctant attendants lowered the convulsing body to the cushions. She lifted his head, sat down on the end and returned it to her lap. Somewhere along the way she had lost her cigarette.

I turned to Clendenan, who had entered on Montana's shambling heels. "Where do you keep the liquor?"

He was watching the wreckage of his father. He gestured vaguely in the direction of a console stereo under the curtained front window. "This is a hell of a time to think about getting pie-eyed."

"Can you think of a better one? Anyway, it's for her."

"I don't want anything," she said petulantly.

"You'll have something. Bourbon do?" I hoisted a well-tapped fifth of Ten High out of the record cabinet and looked around for a glass.

"Have I got a choice?"

The kitchen was almost as big as the living room, a French touch. I splashed some whiskey into a heavy tumbler and drank long and deep. Then I rinsed it out, splashed in more whiskey and water, and brought the glass into the living room, where I pressed it into her hand and closed her fingers around it. "Drink."

She did, sipping at first, the tumbler cupped in both

185

hands, but as the liquid burned her tongue she tilted it higher, too high, so that she choked and began coughing. She had to shove most of her fist into her mouth to stop. I finished my cigarette and watched. She recovered, took another sip, and set the vessel down on a glass-topped coffee table. Her face was flushed.

"Did you ever find the will?"

"The will?" She resumed rocking, cooing to the thing in her lap as if it were a cranky baby. "Oh, that. There never was a will. I made it up."

"You made it up."

Her eyes sought mine. They were slightly out of focus. "I knew Arthur wasn't killed on that fishing trip. Before he left, whenever I brought up the subject, he'd change it. I knew him better than anyone, including his wife." She spat the last word. "I was sure he wasn't planning on going. Afterwards, I started that rumor about a new will because I thought it might open an investigation. I didn't have any evidence that he was still alive, but I thought that if enough people looked into his affairs something might turn up. I didn't count on being ignored by everyone involved."

"You're lying, sister."

She said nothing, just went on rocking. The injured man's face was gray, and his breathing was growing shallow.

"You didn't know if he was dead or alive," I pressed. "You wanted to open an investigation, all right, but you wanted it to show that DeLancey's wife arranged for his death. Why?"

"Because she had it coming."

She'd stopped rocking now, and was looking up at me with a face taut with hatred. Even her eyes couldn't spoil it.

"I was living in an apartment in Grosse Pointe Woods the day Arthur left on that trip. A six-room suite with a live-in maid and a choice view of the lake. The next day I was back on the street. Mrs. DeLancey cut off the rent and told the landlord if I wasn't out of the building by nightfall

186

she'd throw him to her lawyers like a bone. That was when her husband was still considered missing, not dead.''

"When'd you find out he was still alive?"

"I always suspected it. I found out for sure eight months ago, in Tucson."

"What were you doing out in Arizona?"

"Looking for Arthur, what else?" she said. "He was always interested in the West; I figured if he went anywhere it would be there. I hit all the historic spots: Dodge City, Abilene, the Custer battlefield, Tombstone. I showed his picture around all the museums and souvenir shops. Nothing. I was in Old Tucson and almost broke when I saw him."

There was an electric digital clock somewhere in the room. A constant cooking noise, punctuated at regular intervals by soft clicks as the numbers changed, ticking out the Judge's life like a death-watch beetle. Tim and his partner, bodyguards down to their socks, had stationed themselves at both exits. Clendenan stood behind me and to my right. Montana was out of my sight-line, but I could hear his heavy breathing, louder and more regular than De-Lancey's shuddering gasps. Janet Whiting continued.

"They were putting on a show for the tourists, a phony bank robbery with a lot of shooting and men pitching off rooftops. He was standing in the crowd on the other side of the street. He'd darkened his hair and changed his face, but I recognized him. Even forty pounds lighter there was no mistaking him, not for me. When things quieted down finally I hurried over there, but he was already gone. I did some asking around and found out what hotel he was staying at. The clerk there said he'd just checked out to catch a two-thirty flight. I called the airport. The only plane they had leaving at that time was bound for Detroit Metropolitan Airport. I missed it, but I caught the next one. It's taken me this long to track him down. And now—'' She smoothed a hand over his matted hair and lowered her face, her body convulsed with sobs.

"That's because he was lying low in your home town,

afraid someone might recognize him here," I explained. "What made you go to such lengths to find him?"

"I loved him." Her voice was barely audible through the tears.

"Maybe. Or maybe you loved his millions. It doesn't much matter now."

"Why, Mother?"

I looked at Clendenan. His tan eyes were riveted on the woman. She raised her face. Her pretty eyes were red and swollen.

"Why did you tell me there was another will when he never made one out?" he demanded.

"Would you have helped me otherwise?" She watched him levelly. "You didn't inherit many of his qualities, William. Just his faults. Greed especially."

"You bitch!"

"I never pretended to be anything else."

"How did he help you?"

There was a pause. I repeated the question. Clendenan responded hastily.

"I looked into Griffin Carbide's affairs. The union keeps extensive files on all its investments."

"What about Jack Billings?" I was looking at her. "What did he do for you?"

"Jack," she said, smiling wistfully. "Dear Jack. He went through his stepfather's papers, including a few that got mixed up with the inventory of Arthur's firearms collection when he sold it. That was where he found the name of the doctor Arthur had paid to change his face. But by the time he reached him the doctor was long dead. Suicide, the police said. That was a year ago. When I got back from out West I had to start all over again, by talking to Arthur's old acquaintances. It was just a fluke that I remembered his pilot's real name and looked up his brother at The Crescent."

"Why didn't you talk to Montana?"

Her mouth hardened. "Phil was one of the men who would have liked to see Arthur dead. I wasn't going to tell him I thought he was still alive."

188

"That's not true," the union chief protested.

She ignored him. "That's why I called you when I recognized Phil's bodyguard from pictures I'd seen of him in the newspapers, posing as a waiter."

"That, and because you knew Montana had reason to resent your stringing him along to find out what you could about DeLancey's supposed death," I added. "He thought you were after the will, but the result was the same."

She drained the tumbler and put it back on the table. "I'm not denying it," she said. "I'd have done anything to make sure Arthur was safe."

"Anything," I echoed. "Including promising to cut Jack Billings in on the nonexistent inheritance. Manipulating him the way you did Montana and your son. Making the reward seem so sweet that when you dropped out of sight, Billings went out to Huron in the hopes of picking up your trail and wound up killing a private investigator who went out there for the same reason."

She raised her eyebrows, not very far. Her eyes were deep pools of innocence. "I don't know anything about that. Was he a friend of yours?"

"It doesn't much matter. Any man's death diminishes me."

Clendenan looked green. "I'm going to be sick."

"The time for that is past," I snapped. "You had your chance yesterday afternoon, when you killed Krim."

He shifted his attention back to me, and he wasn't green anymore. His face was skull-white.

26

"YOUR TIMING'S GETTING WORSE," SAID THE SECRETARY slowly. "But as long as you've started, you may as well go on to the punch line. You'd better hope I laugh."

His verbiage was pure Warner Brothers, another example of life imitating art. I let my eyes drop to the floor, pretending to be choosing my words. After a moment I located the cord to the lamp where it plugged into the wall. It was good to know for future reference.

"There's a bushel of motives to choose from," I began. "For now I'll stick with the one that's worked so far. You said Krim boasted of having killed Jefferson. I'd call it a progress report. Your mother said the bodyguard's presence worried her, so she called me for protection. Wrong. For that she went to Krim. She couldn't have used the phony will to win him over, because he knew the Judge was still alive and he had a good thing going as it was. My guess is she used those great big baby blues of hers. He was hard, but he wasn't hard enough to resist those.

"She used some story to get Krim to agree to lay a trap for Jefferson, who he probably didn't know from Adam, and then she lured the bodyguard back to her apartment and straight into the Arab's line of fire. If it looked bad to have a stiff in her home, she left little clues to indicate that she hadn't departed voluntarily—her purse, money, and bank book, all her clothes. Why not? She stood to gain far more. I was the clincher. No one who was planning a murder would hire a private investigator to nose around and uncover things—no one, that is, who was less devious than Janet Whiting.''

Montana said, "Why didn't she just have Krim ambush him on the street?''

"No good. She wanted an investigation that would eventually lead back to Leola DeLancey, and to swing that she had to make it look like more than another street killing. How were you going to implicate her, Janet? By getting Jack Billings to plant his stepfather's derringer in her bedroom?''

She daubed at the Judge's quaking face with the blood-soaked handkerchief and pretended not to hear.

"She told me she got off at two," I said to whoever was listening. "The odds are she left at least an hour earlier, to be sure and finish the job and clear out before I showed up. That shouldn't be too hard to check.

"Getting the Arab to do it accomplished two things: It got Jefferson out of her way, and it gave her leverage against the killer. In court it would be her word against his, and he knew what would come of that. He had to let her see DeLancey or go to jail. What happened when they got together, only she knows. It doesn't matter. The point is her plan worked.

"The problem with using a snake to catch a rat is what do you do with the snake afterwards? As long as there was a bare possibility the police might buy Krim's story, he couldn't be left to talk. But a mother can always count on her son." I met the secretary's gaze. "Did you really use a claw hammer?''

He had regained a great deal of his composure, though his complexion was still unhealthy. "What makes you think it wasn't DeLancey?'' he asked. "Blunt objects were no strangers to him.''

"You do. You said he wasn't so good at killing when he was close to his victim. I imagine that was one of the qualities your mother says you didn't inherit. And like all good secretaries you kept a cool head, not forgetting to collect your father's derringer afterwards, so that your mother could carry out the plans she had for it. But you

191

should have taken time to search his office and grab the account book he used to record DeLancey's blackmail payments.''

''Who'd have thought he was stupid enough to bank them?'' Clendenan brought out the little Forehand & Wadsworth.

I fired the .38 through my jacket pocket. He fired at the same time, but his shot went wild and shattered the front window behind me. Then he folded onto his knees and pitched forward, still holding the now-useless single-shot. His mother screamed.

I didn't bother to look and see what the bodyguards were up to. Instead I twirled the lamp cord around my ankle and jerked the china-base lamp off the end table beside Janet Whiting's chair. We both hit the floor at the same time, I rolling, the lamp shattering and plunging the room in darkness. A .45 roared, orange flame slashing the night. I fired at the flash once, twice. I heard a loud grunt. There was another roar from a different quarter. Something hot raked my rib cage. I rolled again and squeezed one off in the direction of a fading phosphorescence. Then I rolled back the other way, an instant before the second .45 opened up again, the bullet slapping the floor where I'd been.

Silence throbbed louder than any of the explosions. I stuck a finger in one ear and waggled it to clear out the wad of noise that was stopping it up. Now I heard the Judge's labored breathing and the digital clock clunking out the minutes.

Some light was leaking in through the broken window. It glinted off a pair of eyeglasses moving beneath the sill. I released two rounds for good measure. There was a gasp and a thud.

Suddenly the room was full of light. I looked up, blinking, at Tim standing beside the wall switch next to the door. One hand was gripping his big automatic, the other his abdomen, where bright arterial blood was squirting between his fingers. I aimed the .38 carefully and squeezed the trigger. The hammer snapped on an empty shell. I tried

192

twice more. Same story. His eyes were wild as he leveled his .45 at me.

The room shook with a fresh explosion. I jerked spasmodically, positive I'd been hit. The towheaded bodyguard held his position a moment longer, seeming to hang there, still pointing the gun. Blood from a huge hole in his left temple drained down his neck into his collar. Then he crumpled into a heap.

I turned my head. Phil Montana stood in front of the window, gripping the other bodyguard's Army Colt. Smoke blurred his image.

The bespectacled guard was sitting on the floor beneath the window with his back propped against the wall, cradling his left arm in his right hand. His jacket sleeve was soaked where one or both of my bullets had shattered the elbow.

Bill Clendenan lay twitching where he had fallen. I couldn't tell if he was alive or if it was just nerves.

On the sofa, the Judge was still gulping air.

I was dimly aware of a keening sound in the distance growing louder. My shirt felt warm and wet. I opened my jacket and looked down to see that it was smeared bright red. I began to lose consciousness.

The last thing I saw before darkness overtook me was Janet Whiting sprawled in an unladylike position on the sofa, her head to one side and a hole in her left breast that could only have been made by a .45. Her eyes had already begun to cloud over.

27

THE NURSE, IF THAT'S WHAT SHE WAS, FROWNED PRET-
tily as she helped me on with my shirt. I was wearing
enough tape around my ribs to star in a remake of *The
Mummy*. Late-morning sunlight bounced perkily off the
pastel walls of my room at Detroit Receiving Hospital.

"Doctor wasn't happy to sign that release order," she
complained. "He wanted to keep you under observation."

"Doctor can take a flying leap at the moon. He'd have
been a lot less happy to face charges of unlawful imprison-
onment." Ignoring the twinge in my right side, I reached
for a cigarette and found my shirt pocket empty. I'd forgotten about having smoked my last. I was still groggy
from the anesthetic.

She glared at me reproachfully. She was a petite blonde
in a pale pink pantsuit and track shoes, and she looked
about fifteen. These days you can't tell the nurses from the
candy stripers, the doctors from the orderlies.

I said, "Don't say I should be grateful to him for pinning
my rib back together. I'll be paying him for it for the next
six months. It isn't as if the bullet was still in there when
he cut me open. And if you try to take me out of here in
a wheelchair—" She stalked out before I could finish.

Lieutenant Fitzroy was waiting for me in the pastel corridor. He was holding his porkpie hat.

"I'm not here to see you, so don't go getting touched,"
he snapped, falling into step beside me. "I had orders to

hang around until Judge DeLancey died, just in case he had anything to say.''

"Fat chance."

"Yeah. The quacks say he checked out ten minutes ago. You and I know he hasn't been around since he took that slug. Cranmer's down there now, hearing in Latin how a tenth of an ounce of lead made spaghetti out of the inside of the old man's skull.''

"What about the others?" I put my hat on and smoothed the brim.

"That bodyguard you shot sang us a pretty aria, which was awful nice of him considering he might lose that left arm. His story checks out with Montana's. The secretary, Clendenan, is still out from the operation, but it looks like he's going to pull through. He'll make a hell of a file clerk up at the Jackson pen. Jesus, that living room was straight out of the last act of something by Shakespeare.''

"How would you know?"

"Smart guy. Just don't forget to drop by headquarters. There's a steno and a tape recorder just dying to meet you. They'd like to put your autograph next to Phil Montana's.''

"Later, if that's all right. After I sleep off the dope.''

"Of course it's all right. We aren't about to give some damned lawyer the chance to say we drugged any of our witnesses." We stopped before the elevators. He pressed the Down button. "You'll never guess what airport they picked up Jack Billings at.''

"Honolulu.''

He stared at me. For once he wasn't smiling. I shrugged, wincing at the sudden pain in my side. "Lucky guess.''

The doors slid open. We stepped aside to let out a frizzy-headed orderly in a white coat pushing an empty gurney. On our way down to the lobby, Fitzroy said: "He's waived extradition and he's on his way back here to sign a confession. Says he didn't mean to shoot the op; the gun went off while he was covering him. Could be. It was a thirty-eight Remington, ninety-two years old, with a shaved hammer and a hair trigger.''

"Have you looked into why DeLancey rented the Kitchner place last year?"

"Not yet. I figure he bought it while he was laying low there to use as a safe house close by if he got hot."

I didn't say anything. He reached out and pressed the Stop button. The car lurched to a halt between floors. He faced me, smiling again, not comfortably.

"Your playing cop got people killed, Walker. The D.A. thinks it'll complicate his cases against Billings and Clendenan if we charge you with obstruction of justice, so we're to lay off. But you better hope you don't get caught spitting on the sidewalk from here on in, because I'll pull so many strings you'll be dancing for the next ten years. Today a letter is going to State Police Headquarters in Lansing about your conduct. It'll go into your file along with all the others. Someday there'll be so many of them they won't be able to squeeze the folder back into the drawer. Which is when you stop being a private investigator in this state. On that day I'll spring for champagne down in the squad room."

"What if I had backed off?" I challenged. "How many more bodies would be clogging up the statistics while Janet Whiting went around covering her tracks and you sat around waiting for warrants?"

"I get it. You're Zorro, right? A guy in a big cape on horseback swinging a sword to help out when the cops fall down."

I said, "No, just a guy earning his living. A woman who called herself Ann Maringer hired me to find her. It doesn't matter that she didn't really want to be found. Every time I take on a job I mortgage a piece of myself to my clients and I can't get it back until it's paid off. I have to do that and yet try not to step on the toes of the people who keep me in business. Sometimes that's impossible. I can't help it; it's the way I operate."

"So you're in it for the money."

I sighed and gave up. "If that's the only way you can handle it."

196

"We want that diamond ring, by the way. Now more than ever, for evidence."

"You know what I want before you get it. Signed by a judge."

"You're a son of a bitch," he said flatly.

"That's my excuse. What's yours?"

We finished the ride in silence. He stayed on after I had alighted. My last impression of him was a smiling face with sparkling eyes just before a group of doctors and nurses entered the car, crowding it from view.

A dark blue Cadillac limousine was parked in the loading zone in front of the entrance as I came out. The rear window hummed down and Phil Montana leaned forward. "Care for a lift?"

"If my car's still in the RenCen lot," I replied.

"There's a beat-up Olds Cutlass there registered to an A. Walker."

I got in beside him. A uniformed chauffeur I didn't recognize was sitting behind the wheel. As we pulled away from the curb I glanced from him to my traveling companion with eyebrows raised. He smiled sadly.

"I stole him this morning from a General Motors vice-president. Seen this?"

He handed me the morning edition of the *News*, folded to the society page. At the top was a two-column picture of Leola DeLancey and her attorney, Daniel Clague, smiling reservedly amidst a crowd on the steps of the City-County Building. DeLancey widow weds lawyer in civil ceremony, proclaimed the headline. The edition would have hit the street before word of last night's doings got out. I gave it back without comment.

"You could at least try to look surprised," said the union chief.

"Why? I knew they had a thing for each other. Maybe she's the reason he was willing to give the Judge advice on how to create a dummy corporation. Only a corporation lawyer would know all the ins and outs."

"Conspiracy to commit fraud is a hell of a risk to take for a woman."

"So's murder. But it's done all the time. With the Judge believed dead, Clague had a clear field. The courts must have come through with that death decree or she'd be guilty of bigamy."

He nodded. "It's on the front page. I wouldn't want to be in their position right about now."

I said nothing. Outside, clouds drifted in front of the sun, casting a gray pall over the city. It looked as if it was getting ready to snow. Michigan, phooey.

"There's one thing I don't understand," he said. "If Janet wasn't being held against her will by DeLancey, why did she leave so that he had to follow her to Clendenan's house?"

"She didn't. That was part of Clendenan's story. I think the Judge had his stroke in the Troy apartment and she got her son to help bring him to Grosse Ile, which was a more secluded place to care for him. DeLancey never did have any flunkies; that was just something Clendenan said to make his story more plausible."

Montana sat absorbing that. He was clean-shaven and looked fresh in a different suit. He had managed to squeeze in a few hours' rest since his ordeal at police headquarters. "Happy?" I asked him.

He looked at me with his hard sad eyes. "Is there any reason I should be, with the closest thing I ever had to a son exposed as a traitor? A woman I cared about killed in the crossfire? My having killed two men?"

"I don't read minds. I can't say how you feel about what happened to the woman or to Clendenan. Or about having killed Tim. But you had plenty of time to prepare yourself before you iced DeLancey."

He was still looking at me, but his eyes were no longer sad. Just hard.

"Maybe you'd care to explain."

I settled back in the seat. "You get a lot of thinking done riding in the back of an ambulance. Crazy thoughts mostly, but once in a while something rational creeps in. Like about how a sick man, still in shock over a trusted employee's treachery, can have the presence of mind to

198

shoot another man who's holding a gun on him. Or how that employee can forget to have his boss frisked when he knows he's in the habit of carrying a gun."

He said nothing. I resumed.

"Clendenan's motives were obvious. He thought there was a will that he could share in, but the only way he could collect was if everyone went on thinking the Judge was dead. So he conveniently overlooked the fact that you were armed. That's the whole reason he took us out there. Which means he had reason to believe you wanted DeLancey dead. It couldn't be that old fraud thing. Too weak. It had to be something else, something that a supposedly faithful union employee like Clendenan might fall privy to. Something like a fraud of your own.

"You never did invest union funds in Griffin Carbide, did you? Or if you did, you didn't sink as much in it as you claimed. Maybe you got your old friend Arthur De-Lancey to issue some phony stock certificates and pocketed the balance. It didn't hurt to stage an angry telephone conversation with the Judge when the so-called merger fell through, so that his stepson could overhear it. It was a sweet deal, but what made it sweeter was your going to jail for assault."

He glanced at the driver, but the soundproof glass partition was in place between the front and rear seats. He relaxed slightly. "Go on."

"It was set up from the beginning. You knew that the scandal would hurt your reputation, possibly cost your union presidency. Anyone else would have been content to give it up for the riches to be gained. But you were too much in love with the power. So you framed an employee with an embezzling rap, maybe with his consent, and slugged him in front of witnesses. The dedicated union man outraged at an attempt to steal bread from the mouths of the rank and file. To top it off you even went to jail. It got you re-elected by a landslide, even if you couldn't do anything about it for a long while.

"Everything went beautifully, especially DeLancey's unexpected disappearance. With him gone the threat of ex-

199

posure was removed. It must have been a hell of a shock when he turned up again. What a break when he pointed what looked like a real gun at you and gave you an excuse to do what you'd been planning ever since you found out he was alive.''

We swung into the parking lot at the Renaissance Center. My car was parked where I had left it the day before. As we drew to a stop, a large crowd of men that had been clustered around the entrance to the building surged toward us. The group had grown since the previous night. There was an occasional picket sign, but most of these had been cast into a heap at the foot of the stairs leading up to ground level. They had recognized the limo.

''Your theory's interesting,'' said Montana, as the chauffeur got out to open my door. ''But without evidence that's all it is, a theory. If what you say is true, only Bill Clendenan could have backed it up. He's been exposed as a murderer. Nothing he says is worth anything.''

We stared at each other. The windows were full of rough-hewn faces, the air alive with voice shouting Montana's name. By now they had heard the early radio reports and were aware that their leader had in eliminating his secretary cut loose one of the men upon whom they blamed their troubles. He was their hero still.

''Good-bye, Mr. Walker,'' he said.

I climbed out. The chauffeur snicked the door shut and got back under the wheel. A path opened up before me—I had been riding with the boss, after all—and closed behind my heels, filling up with bodies. It was past eleven-thirty. I had a telephone call to make, if Maggie was in the office. I watched the Cadillac purr away in the direction of the tiered garage, the crowd sprinting alongside it like Romans around a returning emperor's chariot.

They kept chanting Phil Montana's name in cadence.

About the Author

Loren D. Estleman is a graduate of Eastern Michigan University and a veteran police-court journalist. Since the publication of his first novel in 1976, he has established himself as a leading writer of both mystery and western fiction. His western novels include Golden Spur Award winner ACES AND EIGHTS, MISTER ST. JOHN, and THE STRANGLERS. ANGEL EYES is the second book in his Amos Walker mystery series, following MOTOR CITY BLUE. SUGARTOWN, the fifth book in the series, was presented the Shamus Award for Best Private Eye Novel of the Year by Private Eye Writers of America. Estleman lives in Whitmore Lake, Michigan.